jF PARKS Tiffany
Midnight in the piazza /
Parks, Tiffany,

Midnight in the Piazza

Tiffany Parks

HARPER
An Imprint of HarperCollinsPublishers

Midnight in the Piazza
Text copyright © 2018 by Tiffany Parks
Illustrations by Becca Stadtlander
All rights reserved. Printed in the United States of America.
No part of this book may be used or reproduced in any manner whatsoever
without written permission except in the case of brief quotations embodied
in critical articles and reviews. For information address HarperCollins
Children's Books, a division of HarperCollins Publishers, 195 Broadway,
New York, NY 10007.
www.harpercollinschildrens.com

Library of Congress Control Number: 2017939002
ISBN 978-0-06-264452-7

Typography by Torborg Davern
18 19 20 21 22   CG/LSCH   10 9 8 7 6 5 4 3 2 1

First Edition

In loving and joyful memory of
my father, Sam Parks.

one

A LITTLE CHANGE

He might as well have told her they were moving to Antarctica.

It was a month to the day after Beatrice Archer's thirteenth birthday when her dad made the fatal announcement. Once he'd broken the news, she felt as if someone had yanked out her guts and baked them into a pie.

It was a shame, really, because the day had started out so perfectly—as promising as a stack of brand-new books, their spines uncreased and their pages just waiting for a pair of greedy eyes. It was one of those crisp, bright New England mornings when the chill tickles your nose but the budding magnolia trees promise spring is just around the corner.

Beatrice trotted down the broad Bostonian avenue after her Saturday-morning flute lesson, her instrument case *clack-clack*ing from its handle like her dad's old-fashioned typewriter. The sound made her feel as alive as if it had been her own heartbeat.

She turned the corner and climbed the stoop of a narrow brownstone, then raced to the top floor to find her dad. Augustus Archer was a history professor, and when he wasn't in the classroom or the Boston Public Library, there was one place in the world his daughter could always find him: his study. It was a cozy room paneled in dark wood with a bay window and floor-to-ceiling shelves heaving with books. Beatrice hadn't read them *all*, but not for lack of trying.

She burst into the study to find her father bent over an enormous tome, a pair of half-moon spectacles balancing on the tip of his nose.

"Hey, Dad."

No answer.

"Dad . . . ?"

Silence.

"Dad!"

Mr. Archer looked up with a start. "Oh, you're home. How was your lesson, sweet pea?"

"Fine." She shook her head with a silent laugh. When her dad was researching he was dead to the world. You could walk into his study with your pants on fire and he wouldn't notice. But it was what made Dad Dad, so Beatrice didn't hold it against him.

"Listen, Bea," he said, closing the book. "There's something I've been wanting to talk to you about." His eyes flicked to a framed photograph of a dark-haired woman, as if he expected her to offer advice or reassurance. Whichever he was seeking, he wasn't likely to get it; it was Beatrice's mother, and she'd been dead for over a decade. With a sniff of resolve, he took Beatrice's hands. "I have big news," he said. He wore a wide grin, but a hint of unease lurked behind his gray eyes.

"We're going to Rome," he announced. Beatrice's eyes widened, but before she had a chance to interrupt, he clarified, "Not for a vacation, but to live, *indefinitely*. I've been offered a position as head of the history department at the American Academy in Rome, plus unlimited access to some of the most restricted libraries in the world. I've given it a good deal of thought over the past few weeks, and I've decided it's too great an opportunity to pass up—for both of us. You'll finish the school year; we'll pack up the house and fly to Rome sometime this summer."

Beatrice stood stock-still, mouth parted in disbelief. For a moment time stopped; then her world began to crumble. Images of friends, home, school, life as she knew it, all disintegrated like confetti in a rainstorm. Three little words surfaced in her brain and she grabbed at them as if to a lifeline: "I'm not going."

"Nonsense! Just think of it: pasta, gelato, the Colosseum! What's not to love?"

"I'm NOT GOING," she repeated, and her mouth hardened into a line.

Being the only child of an older-than-average father, Beatrice Archer was used to getting her own way. Her mass of frizzy hair was obstinately red, and her personality matched it. Her skin may have been fair, with a redhead's unavoidable sprinkling of freckles, but her hazel eyes darkened to brown when she was determined, which was often. Her dad liked to joke that she had him wrapped around her little finger— but this time he wouldn't budge.

"I'm sorry, my dear, but we're moving whether you like it or not," he informed her in his no-arguing voice.

An image flashed before Beatrice's eyes: she was sitting in a classroom full of strangers, all speaking a language she couldn't understand. They were pointing at her and laughing. Her face burned at the thought. The idea of changing schools or cities was bad enough, but changing countries? Changing worlds, more like. Leaving behind her best friend, Georgette; her pet turtles, Nick and Nora; her flute teacher; and everything else she loved about her life in Boston . . .

No, she couldn't—she *wouldn't* let this happen.

At first she tried to be reasonable, outlining the pros and cons of his catastrophic plan, just like her debate coach had taught her. When that didn't work, she threatened a hunger strike. He called her bluff. At one point she stormed out of the room and slammed the door, only to skulk back in on the verge of tears. She tried every tactic, but nothing worked.

Exhausted and losing hope, she collapsed onto the couch, with nowhere to turn but the simple truth. "I don't want to go," she whimpered.

Her dad knelt down, smoothed her bushy hair, and kissed her forehead. "This is going to be a life-altering experience," he whispered, his voice tinged with drama.

"I like my life the way it is *now*."

"Don't be afraid of a little change, sweet pea," he chided.

"A *little* change?" She sat up with a start. "Everything's going to change!"

"It's going to be wonderful," he insisted. "Once you settle in, you'll love it; I promise." When she didn't seem convinced, he asked with a wink, "Have I ever been wrong?"

She narrowed her eyes dubiously.

He continued, undaunted. "We'll be delving into the unknown, *and* we'll have each other. Now, let's get out the map of Rome and decide which *rione* we want to live in!"

"*Rione?*"

"The *rioni* are twenty-two neighborhoods that make up the center of Rome. Each one has its own symbol and history."

In spite of herself, Beatrice was intrigued. Maps, symbols, history: three of her favorite things. Did she really have her dad wrapped around her little finger, or was it the other way around?

Over the following weeks, Beatrice pored over maps and books about Rome. Her dad had spent a few years there before Beatrice was born and was a fountain of knowledge about the place. She tried to imagine him a few decades younger—with red hair like hers—sipping a cappuccino in a sun-soaked piazza, but she couldn't picture it. The dad she knew had tufty white hair and a crinkly face, wore reading glasses that were constantly sliding down his nose, and had a fondness for bow ties and tweed. He spent his days inside, lost in a book or scribbling away on some obscure topic. He was about as far removed from her foggy idea of Rome as you could get.

But as he regaled her with fascinating facts and tidbits of history, little by little she soaked up his enthusiasm.

"Just about everywhere you turn are ancient ruins," he told her, his eyes on fire, "sometimes just lying around, as if no one has touched them in centuries. The same street you take to get to school might have been walked down by Renaissance princes, medieval peasants, even Julius Caesar himself!"

Beatrice's imagination took wing. She'd inherited her dad's love of history, a fascination for the stories of people who'd lived long before her own time. For her, history was even better than fiction; these people had *actually* lived, with dreams and fears and hobbies and best friends, just like she had. Only they'd lived hundreds—even thousands—of years before. Every time she opened a history book or listened to one of her father's stories, she took a step back in time.

What would it be like to live in a place where history wasn't just shut up in books, but living and breathing in the very paving stones you walked on?

two

THE TURTLE FOUNTAIN

The taxi screeched to a halt in a small piazza in a neighborhood known as the Jewish Ghetto. The door swung open and Beatrice clambered out. She spun around, taking in her surroundings.

The buildings were painted in pastels, like different flavors in an ice cream shop. Soot-colored cobblestones shimmered beneath her feet and the shop signs were covered in incomprehensible words. A couple of kids kicked around a soccer ball and an old man sat on a bench, a black cat circling his ankles. She felt a rising sense of delight with her new neighborhood, but underneath sat a brick of anxiety. Was it just fear of the unknown? Fear of change, as her father had chided her?

The splashing of water caught her attention. In the middle of the piazza, a fountain sparkled in the sunlight. Beatrice stared at it, transfixed, drinking in every detail: a pool of turquoise water, massive marble seashells, four laughing boys sculpted in bronze riding miniature dolphins, a basin overflowing above their heads. It was the most perfect fountain she'd ever seen, but the best part were the four bronze turtles that perched on the very top, as if scrambling up to take a drink. They made her think of her pet turtles back in Boston—a bittersweet reminder of the life she'd left behind.

Her dad elbowed her in the ribs, shattering the spell. "Come on, we can sightsee later. We've got unpacking to do and a new home to explore."

Beatrice tore her eyes from the fountain. "Which building's ours, Dad?"

"That one." He pointed up. "Our apartment's on the top floor."

The four-story building was the color of ripe apricots, its deep green shutters closed against the baking sun. A mass of purple flowers exploded over the door-way and tiny white jasmine blossoms crept up the walls. The double front doors—big enough to let in a school bus—were marred with squiggles of graffiti. Beatrice's dad clucked with disapproval as he turned a key in the lock.

They lugged their suitcases inside and climbed into an ancient-looking elevator. As the tiny cabin began its rickety ascent, Beatrice could see the floors they were passing through the grille on the door.

Once they were safely on the top floor, her dad pulled out a key as long as an unsharpened pencil. *Clack, clack, clack, clack.* It turned in the lock four times and the door swung open. Beatrice crossed the threshold with a flutter in her stomach and stepped into a shadowy corridor.

"Here's your room," he said, opening the second door on the right. He strode across the room and flung open the shutters. "Look, you have a view of the fountain!"

"I do?" Beatrice ran to the window and leaned out. Seen from above, the bronze turtles seemed to hover over the lip of the fountain's upper basin. She felt an odd tug at her heart, as if something about this strange new place had been calling to her from across the world.

"So, what do you think?"

"I . . . ," she began, then paused. "I suppose it'll do," she allowed with a wry smile.

Mr. Archer laughed and tousled her hair.

"Dad," she said hesitantly, "why do they call this neighborhood a ghetto?" The only "ghettos" she'd ever heard of were the dangerous neighborhoods in big cities.

"Because this is where the word comes from. The ghettos you're thinking of took their names from Italian ghettos like this one, but the meaning changed along the way."

"So . . ." She waited for him to elaborate. "What does it mean?"

Augustus Archer had a way of explaining things without actually explaining anything. When Beatrice showed interested in a topic, he'd pique her curiosity, then leave her to do the digging. She'd learned the art of researching at his knee and spent many an afternoon in the Boston Public Library puzzling out a mystery.

"*Ghetto* is a word for an area of a city where people of a certain ethnicity or background live. Some people think it came from the Italian word *borghetto*, which means 'little town.' For centuries, the Jews of Rome were confined to this neighborhood. It was the only place they could live—and it wasn't pleasant. Many were forced to live in squalor, abide by curfews, work demeaning jobs."

The blood in her veins turned to ice water.

"The walls of the Ghetto and many of its buildings were torn down a century and a half ago," he continued, "but the ironic thing is, today this neighborhood is considered one of the loveliest in the city, and now everyone wants to live here. Of course, the Jewish-Roman population still lives and thrives here."

"But why were they *forced* to live here? Who would do such a thing?"

Her father sighed. "Ah, my dear, history has more than its share of barbaric chapters."

Beatrice's ears perked up, ready for a juicy story.

Her father patted her head distractedly. "I'm exhausted from that all-night flight, and you must be too." Beatrice's shoulders slumped. "How about you try to sleep off some of that jet lag?"

With her curiosity whetted, she knew sleep would not come easily. But in spite of herself, her eyelids were drooping. Maybe, after a long nap, she'd be able to do some digging.

three

THE WINDOW THAT
WASN'T THERE

Hunger woke her. After sleeping for what felt like days, Beatrice rolled over with a pang in her stomach. Her eyes struggled to take in her surroundings, but the room was nearly pitch-black. Slowly, a faint light appeared around the window shutters and the objects in the room began to take shape. It all came rushing back to her: she was in Rome.

With a tightening in the pit of her stomach, she slipped out of bed and stumbled toward the open window, feeling her way across the dark room. After fumbling with the unfamiliar latch, she unfastened the shutters and pushed them out into the night. They opened with a satisfying creak.

The city was asleep. She wondered what time it was back home.

Home. What was Georgette doing right now? Was she taking good care of Beatrice's turtles? Had she already found a new best friend?

Looking down at the fountain that had enchanted her by daylight, Beatrice felt only loneliness, worlds away from her familiar life. Her stomach growled. How long had she slept? It could have been ten p.m. or four in the morning for all she could tell.

She found the switch and the room flooded with light. She had to admit, her new bedroom was pretty fantastic. Wooden beams painted with blue flowers, green garlands, and gold swirls crisscrossed the high ceiling. The rust-colored terra-cotta tiles were cool under her bare feet, despite the summer heat. A rickety spiral staircase led to a loft above her bed, suspended halfway between the floor and the ceiling: a space just big enough for a desk and chair.

But despite the charm and novelty of her new digs, they weren't home. She missed her old room, its soft, squishy carpet, her rows of dog-eared paperbacks, her familiar, comfy bed. This place didn't even have a closet! Just a puny little wardrobe that looked like it would topple over if you put in more than a week's worth of clothes.

She eyed the open suitcases and their contents strewn across the floor. The prospect of finding a new home for each and every object filled her with dread. Unlike her father, organization was not her strong suit. She gave it up as a lost cause and went to close the shutters, taking one last peek at the gurgling fountain below.

A dim streetlamp burned in the corner of the piazza and a spotlight illuminated the fountain, but not a single light came from the dozens of other windows facing the square.

Except . . . across the piazza stood a white building, directly opposite her own. Beatrice squinted at a small window on the second floor. No light came from it, yet somehow a shadow seemed to hover there. She knew better than to look in other people's windows, but something about this one was definitely odd.

She switched off her light and dug in her carry-on

for the travel binoculars she'd brought for studying church ceilings. She crouched on the floor and peeked over the windowsill.

Peering at the white building through the binoculars, she discovered that the window wasn't a window at all. At least, not anymore. There was no glass inside the frame, just a walled-up space with painted-on windowpanes. And yet—impossibly—an indistinct shape quivered there, like a silhouette behind a curtain. Beatrice's heartbeat quickened.

She placed the binoculars on the sill and scanned the square. A black cat stood on the brim of the fountain, stretching languidly. As it did, the shape on the walled-up window distorted. The cat hopped to the ground, out of the beam of the fountain's spotlight, and the mysterious shape disappeared.

Beatrice exhaled. It was just the shadow of a cat. She chided herself for being silly and reached out to pull in the shutters. Just then, a pair of sneakers *squish-squish*ed across the cobblestones below.

A young man stalked across the otherwise motionless square. He was tall and lanky with a shaved head and tattoos snaking down his arms, a backpack slung over one shoulder. With every few steps he whipped his head around, as if he were afraid someone was following him.

As he crept in the direction of Beatrice's building, she yanked in the shutters. The squeal of the unoiled hinges echoed through the square and the man looked up just as the shutters slammed into place.

Had he seen her?

Beatrice peered down through the shutter's wooden slats, but the man was out of sight. She couldn't see him without reopening the shutters and sticking her head out, and she wasn't about to do that.

What was he up to? Maybe *he* was the vandal who'd scribbled graffiti on her front door, and was back at it again? Or worse, maybe he was trying to break into one of the buildings in the piazza!

She strained her ears. Nothing.

For a moment she thought about waking her father, but no, she was probably just jumping to conclusions. Her dad was always teasing her, saying she had an overactive imagination and a naturally suspicious character. The guy on the street below was likely as harmless as a fruit fly.

"Mind your own business, Bea," she advised herself. Able to resist her hunger pangs no longer, she put the man with the shaved head out of her mind and went in search of her new kitchen and, with any luck, a satisfying snack.

Over the next few days, between unpacking and sleeping off jet lag, Beatrice and her dad found slivers of time to visit Rome's major sites. But soon Mr. Archer consigned himself to the library, determined to get a head start on his research before classes began in the fall. Beatrice was used to her dad's frequent absences. Still, she wasn't about to sit around indoors—she had a city to explore.

"I don't like the idea of you out roaming all by yourself," said her dad one morning as she prepared to take a walk.

"You never worried about it in Boston. Do you think we should have stayed instead of moving to Rome?" Beatrice teased.

"Just promise you'll keep your wits about you! Do you have your cell phone? Is it charged?"

"Of course!" She tapped the disappointingly low-tech hand-me-down phone in her pocket.

"And don't forget your map. You know our address, right?"

"Ye-es," she sang impatiently. "Piazza Mattei, 10."

"Don't talk to *any* strangers—"

Beatrice rolled her eyes. "You taught me that when I was six. I'll be smart."

He took her by the shoulders, his pale gray eyes piercing her hazel ones. "You're not in your home country anymore," he said gravely. "Some people take advantage of foreigners, and it's easy to get distracted. I know you'll be fine, but just don't let your guard down, okay?"

"I promise," she said with equal seriousness.

"Have fun, then, princess." He mussed her copper locks. "Or perhaps I should say, *principessa!*"

four

EXPLORATIONS AND EMBARRASSING SITUATIONS

Stepping into the morning sun felt as soft and delicious as slipping into a warm bath. The neighborhood was just waking up: a motor scooter buzzed past, cups rattled on saucers in a nearby café, and a woman's high heels *clack-clack-clack*ed across the cobblestones.

No sooner had the enormous door of her building swung shut behind her than Beatrice's gaze fell upon the babbling fountain in the center of the piazza. She felt an overpowering pull toward it, as if an invisible string attached to the foot of one of the turtles was fastened to her sternum. Maybe it was just that the turtles reminded her of her pets back home, or perhaps it was the way the gleeful look on the faces of the sculpted boys buoyed her own spirits. Whatever it was, the turtle fountain was officially her favorite thing in Rome.

She picked a direction at random and skirted down an alley, shadowy and deserted. Via di Sant'Ambrogio read a sign on the wall of a building. A laundry line hung across the narrow street with a row of pink baby clothes, but apart from this fresh sign of life, everything else belonged to the past: worn paving stones, narrow arched windows, massive wooden doors with lion's-head knockers. She half expected someone dressed in Renaissance finery to come prancing through a doorway.

The alley opened onto a wide, busy street. Here, modern life was bustling all around: people scurrying about with shopping bags, old men arguing and gesticulating, elderly ladies gossiping on benches. Beatrice's eyes danced between silver menorahs sparkling in a shopwindow, an enormous stack of laundry detergent boxes teetering outside a corner market, and a wicker basket overflowing with purple artichokes sitting in front of a restaurant.

Then she stopped in her tracks. An ancient building with crumbling brick walls and cracked marble columns stood at the end of the street. Beatrice knew these sites were called ruins, but she didn't like the term. She didn't think they were ruined at all. The fact that they were still standing, after so many centuries, made them *un*ruined somehow.

The decrepit building looked as wobbly as a house of cards. Disintegrating columns and a brick arch supported a marble slab with an illegible inscription. A few columns sprouted from the nearby sidewalk, as if refusing to give up their ground to the modern city.

As Beatrice approached the crumbling mass of stone, she tried to visualize what it had looked like two thousand years ago, with columns intact and walls gleaming with marble, maybe even bronze. She imagined that the handful of tourists in pastel polo shirts and khaki shorts, snapping pictures and thumbing through guidebooks, were ancient Romans in togas instead, going about their business and chattering away in Latin.

How many people, throughout the centuries, had stood where she was standing now, gazing up at this same building? If she only knew what it was . . .

As if in answer to this silent wish, a slender young man with floppy brown hair and a crisp white shirt sauntered over. A few dozen tourists straggled behind him, gazing at the monument with varying degrees of interest.

"And this, ladies and gentlemen, is the Portico of Octavia!" he announced in a hoity-toity British accent. He paused for effect, but no one in the group seemed to have heard of it. Beatrice's ears perked up as he started what sounded like a well-rehearsed speech.

"Shortly before Augustus became emperor, when he was still known by his birth name Octavian, he built this structure in honor of his sister, Octavia. The Romans weren't very creative when it came to naming their children," he added parenthetically. He paused, as if he'd just said something fantastically witty, but instead of a laugh, his group rewarded him with a collective blank stare. "Anyway," he continued, "built on the foundations of an earlier portico . . ."

Beatrice slipped into the group, hoping to pass for one of the tourists. She pulled out her trusty notebook and began taking notes, jotting down the purpose, date, and materials of the portico so she could check the tour guide's facts as soon as she got home.

When he finished his speech, he began herding the group to the right. Beatrice turned and gasped. Between a few buildings, she caught a glimpse of another ancient site just beyond: a gigantic, curving structure with three levels of arches and columns.

"The Colosseum!" Beatrice shouted involuntarily. She immediately regretted it. Everyone in the group spun around to gawk at her, then turned back to look at the monument in question.

The guide wore a look of condescending amusement. "No, little girl," he snorted, "that's not the Colosseum. It's the Theater of Marcellus!"

A few of the tourists chuckled at her mistake, as if they'd known all along it was the theater of old what's-his-face.

"I suppose it might be confused with the Colosseum to the *uneducated* eye," the guide allowed with a sniff, flicking his hair out of his eyes.

Beatrice's face burned to the roots of her hair. She wished she could just disappear. Or maybe turn into a column herself.

"I'm sorry," the guide said smugly, "I don't remember seeing you at the sign-up for this tour. Are you part of this group?"

It wasn't enough that he'd laughed at her in front of everyone; now he was exposing her as a shameless eavesdropper. If only she'd listened casually from the side, she might have gone unnoticed, but she'd planted herself in the middle of the group and now she had no excuse.

"Um . . ." Her mouth went dry. "I got a little bit lost. . . ." She pulled out her phone and tapped a few keys at random. "My dad's probably wondering where I am. I should . . ." Without finishing the sentence, she turned and bolted, desperate to put as much space as possible between her and the source of her humiliation.

She hadn't gone a dozen paces when her right foot landed on a wobbly cobblestone. The toe of her flip-flop embedded itself in a crevice, sending her flying. She landed on all fours, her nose inches from the smooth gray stones, with an ominous *crunch* from the hand that held her cell phone. Before she had time to register any pain, a hot rush of blood surged to her face.

"You see that, everyone?" floated a smug voice from behind her. "Remember what I told you about Roman cobblestones? They bruise like murder, but they never break the skin. Marvelous invention."

Beatrice looked down to inspect the damage. Her bare knees, wrists, and palms ached, but sure enough, there wasn't a scratch on her. The same could not be said for her shattered phone. Her dad would be livid. She suddenly hated each Roman cobblestone with every fiber of her being.

Ignoring her throbbing knees, she scooped up the remains of her phone, scrabbled to her feet, and forced herself to walk down the street without limping. Desperate for escape, she stepped blindly into the first open shop.

Once inside, she peeked around the corner, but the guide had moved on and was leading the group toward the Theater of Marcellus. She'd never mistake it for the Colosseum again as long as she lived, she vowed, rubbing her tender palms.

She straightened her shirt as a deliciously familiar smell filled her nostrils.

five

A RELUCTANT NEWBIE

In her haste to escape the scene of her humiliation, Beatrice had inadvertently wandered into an American bakery, right in the middle of Rome. A batch of freshly baked chocolate-chip cookies had just come out of the oven. Things were looking up.

The price of two euros for one medium-sized cookie was a bit shocking. Still, she *had* to have that cookie, whatever the cost. She deserved it after being laughed at by a group of strangers, not to mention having her phone ground to pieces.

She scrounged in her bag for the necessary coins and handed them over in exchange for a warm, moist piece of heaven. She closed her eyes and bit into it, the sensations of home flooding over her. It was as if she were no longer on a crowded street in Rome, but back in Boston, sitting at her own kitchen table. At that moment she would have traded all the marvels of Europe to be sitting at that table, sharing her cookie with Georgette.

Tears welled up in her eyes, but she wiped them away before they could fall. She wasn't going to let the shop assistant see her crying over a chocolate-chip cookie. She sniffed a couple of times, hoping to pass for someone with allergies, and began retracing her steps back to the apartment that was now her home.

She turned the corner into a small piazza. Three boys about her age were kicking around a soccer ball. This was already a regular sight, but something was different about these kids—something familiar.

"Sean, over here!" shouted the tallest boy.

English! They were American! An irrepressible urge to talk to them—to communicate with other kids in her own language—washed over her. She summoned all her courage and when the ball rolled her way, she stopped it with her foot and said, "Hi. I'm Beatrice. Where're you guys from?"

She felt idiotic even as she said it. Couldn't she have thought up anything more clever to say?

"We're from the States," the tallest boy said. "I'm Alex. I'm from California, and Sean and Kevin are from Michigan. But we live here." He seemed proud of this fact, although he was clearly trying to act like it was no big deal.

"Yeah, I live here too," said Beatrice, attempting to match his coolness. "But I'm from Boston originally." She'd heard people drop in the word *originally* when referring to their hometowns, and thought it sounded sophisticated.

"Cool."

"Do you guys live in this neighborhood?"

Before they could answer, another boy came jogging up. With his brown curly hair, olive skin, and trendy clothes, he looked more like the local kids.

"*Ciao, rega'!*"[1] he called to the American boys.

"*Ciao, Marco!*" they answered, slapping each other's hands.

"*È un'amica vostra?*"[2] said the boy called Marco, glancing at Beatrice.

. . . .

1. "Hey, guys!"
2. "Is she a friend of yours?"

"*No, è un'americana che vive qui,*"[3] explained the boy called Sean.

Beatrice's eyes widened. He spoke perfect Italian! How long had he lived here to be able to speak like that?

"*L'abbiamo appena conosciuta,*"[4] added Alex.

Beatrice had no idea what they were saying, but she knew it was about her. As if on cue, she flushed scarlet. It was a redhead's curse, and she was powerless to stop it.

"*Piacere,*"[5] said Marco to Beatrice with a winning smile, each cheek pierced by a dimple. "*Da quanto tempo stai qua?*"[6]

Beatrice's stomach wobbled as a pair of liquid brown eyes stared into hers. She ransacked her brain for a snippet of Italian small talk, but anything she attempted would have given her away as an imposter.

After a few moments' silence, which felt like an eternity, Alex said with an accusatory tone, "I thought you said you lived here! And you can't even speak Italian?"

. . . .

3.   "Not really, she's an American who lives here."
4.   "We just met her."
5.   "Nice to meet you."
6.   "How long have you lived here?"

Beatrice felt like a fraud. But she did live here! She hadn't been lying.

She swallowed. "Well, we only just moved here earlier this summer." *This summer* sounded a lot better than *last week*. "I haven't had time to learn any Italian yet." She tried not to sound defensive.

"Oh, a newbie! Ha-ha! We'll see how you adjust!" Alex kicked the ball out from under Beatrice's foot. The boys took up their game and she was instantly forgotten. Refusing to give them the satisfaction of showing off their soccer skills, she stalked away without another word.

"But you only just got here! It's not easy to adjust to a new city, let alone a new country," said her dad after she'd described her humiliating day. "Don't be so hard on yourself, Bea. You'll get the hang of it."

"I'm not so sure," she muttered. "It seems like everything in this city was designed to make me feel like a complete idiot. I can't even communicate. Do you know how frustrating that is?" She slumped onto the couch.

"As a matter of fact, I do. But you'll learn the language in no time. I have a feeling you're going to be a natural."

Beatrice rolled her eyes. Why was he always so infernally optimistic? "I'll be the only one in my class who can't speak Italian. How embarrassing!"

"But you'll be attending international school; your classes and homework will be entirely in English."

"Still! If all the kids speak Italian except for me, then every time they do, I'll just have to stand there like a moron." Her cheeks flushed at the thought. *I'll be left out*, she wanted to add, but it sounded too pathetic to say out loud.

"I've got it!" her dad exclaimed. "I'll hire you an Italian tutor—just for the summer—to come for a few hours each morning and give you private lessons. By the time school starts, you'll be speaking Italian as well as Dante himself!"

Oh, great. Now on top of everything else, she was being condemned to summer school. *Private* summer school.

"Why didn't I think of this before? There's a retired university professor living in this building. I'll ask her if she knows a good tutor, and with any luck, you can start first thing Monday."

Beatrice groaned silently. She couldn't complain, not after the fuss she'd made. And who knew? Maybe she *would* be a natural, like her dad said. Maybe after a few lessons, she'd be able to show the neighborhood boys just how fast she could learn a new language.

Mr. Archer was true to his word, and the following Monday morning, with a lump in her throat, Beatrice was waiting for her tutor to arrive for their first lesson. What if she couldn't remember the words? What if she couldn't even pronounce them?

The buzzer sounded, scattering Beatrice's negative thoughts. She opened the door to find a young woman with dark bobbed hair, an oval face, and an aquiline nose. She wore a severe black suit and stood as straight as a Corinthian column. Her appearance was animated by two black eyes glittering behind a pair of green-rimmed glasses.

"Hello," said Beatrice, holding the door wide. "I'm Beatrice. Come in." She managed a smile despite her nerves.

"*Piacere*," said her new tutor, shaking Beatrice's hand in a businesslike manner. "*Io mi chiamo Ginevra Furbetta.*"[7]

. . . .

7.   "My name is Ginevra Furbetta."

Beatrice froze, the smile dying on her lips. She realized with dismay that she didn't even know the Italian for *Pardon me?*

"*Piacere*," Ginevra repeated pointedly.

"Ah, right, *piacere*." Beatrice parroted. She'd read this word in her phrase book. It meant *Nice to meet you*. Maybe she'd get the hang of this after all. "Please, come in—"

"*Solo italiano!*" Ginevra cut her off sternly.

Beatrice stared unblinking.

"Only Italian. No Eengleesh!" her new teacher admonished.

Oh. No. She could barely say a word! How had she gotten herself into this mess?

Ginevra followed a perturbed Beatrice into the dining room. She smiled and sat down at the table, pulling out a notebook and pencil. Beatrice slid into the chair beside her, her ears turning pink in anticipation of her inevitable humiliation.

"*Allora,*" Ginevra chirped, "*cominciamo.*"[8]

Despite not understanding, Beatrice liked hearing Ginevra speak. The Italian words danced off her

. . . .

8. "Now then, let's begin."

tongue like a melody on a flute.

"*Io mi chiamo Ginevra.*"[9] The tutor indicated herself, placing her left hand on her chest, and wrote the words out in a notebook.

Beatrice was surprised how it was spelled; the *ch* of *chiamo* made a *k* sound. If they wanted a *k* sound, why didn't they just put a *k* in there?

"*Tu ti chiami Beatrice,*"[10] Ginevra continued. Except she pronounced the name in an entirely different way; it sounded like *Bay-ah-tree-chay*. Beatrice didn't recognize her own name until she saw it written on the page.

"Beatrice," she said slowly so her teacher would know how to pronounce it.

"*No,*" corrected Ginevra, "*Bay-ah-tree-chay.*" As Ginevra stressed the *tree* sound, she rolled the *r* a little, like the flutter of a bird's wings. It sounded exotic, like a line from an opera, but it wasn't her name. "*In italiano, il tuo nome è Be-a-tri-ce,*"[11] Ginevra insisted.

Beatrice had a feeling she wasn't going to win this argument, so she did her best, and stammered out a

· ·

9. "My name is Ginevra."
10. "Your name is Beatrice."
11. "In Italian, your name is Beatrice."

hopeful "*Io mi chiamo Bay-ah-tree-chay.*" She spoke each syllable slowly, struggling to pronounce them just as Ginevra had.

"*Brava,*" her teacher said with a curt nod of approval.

Beatrice raised an incredulous eyebrow. Was she teasing her? *Brava* was something you shouted to prima donnas at the opera house, not beginner language students. But Ginevra had a straight face.

"*Be-a-tri-ce,*" she repeated again. She was beginning to like the way her name sounded in Italian.

They managed to get through the two-and-a-half-hour lesson without speaking a word of English. Beatrice was often tempted to do so, but Ginevra was strict about the no-English rule. By the end of the lesson, Beatrice's head was spinning with all the new information she'd just crammed inside. She noted down her homework assignment and escorted her teacher to the door.

As she gathered her things, Ginevra glanced around the apartment appraisingly. Her eyes lingered on the view through the living room windows and she wandered over to gaze into the piazza.

"What a lov-eh-lee view you have," she remarked, in thickly accented English.

"You speak English!"

"Of course I speak Eengleesh! But I am your Italian tutor, and during lessons we must nat-ural-lee speak only in Italian." She paused, a gleam in her black eye. "But the lesson ees over now."

Beatrice felt duped. She imagined how silly she must have looked, pantomiming words to avoid saying them in English.

Ginevra continued to stare out the window. An impish smile played at the corners of her lips, as if she had a secret but wasn't going to share it. "Thees ees a very special fountain. You are fortunate to be able to see eet every day."

"I know. I fell in love with it the first moment I saw it."

"It has that effect on people. According to legend, eet was built een just one night."

"One night? That's impossible!"

"That ees what they say," she said in a dreamy voice. Then she snapped back to reality. "Who knows? In Roma, anything ees possible."

Tongue-tied, Beatrice stared down at the fountain. By the time she'd gathered her wits and turned to ask her more about it, Ginevra was already gliding out the door.

six

SEEKING, SEARCHING, SKETCHING

Beatrice stared out the window, as if in a trance.

A legend. There was a legend behind the fountain. Her stomach fluttered with glee. She had to find out everything about it.

She skipped into her father's meticulously organized study and scanned the items on his desk: sharpened pencils lined up in a tray, a stack of monogrammed stationery, a notepad, an Olivetti typewriter that was older than she was, and a newspaper, read and refolded. On one corner of the desk sat a few framed photographs of a smiling flame-haired child at various ages, as well as one of a striking brunette. Her mother.

Beatrice stopped in front of the picture. She'd seen it hundreds of times before. It had occupied her father's desk in Boston for as long as she could remember, but even so, it made her pause.

She knew next to nothing about her mother. Only that her name was Isabella and that she'd died of a sudden illness two weeks after Beatrice's second birthday. Common sense told her she couldn't miss someone she couldn't remember, but she missed her all the same. Despite the love she got from her dad, there were places in her heart—deep, inscrutable crevices— that only a mother's love could reach, and sometimes she felt hers were covered in cobwebs.

She ached to know more about her, but she'd learned long ago not to bother asking her dad. Whenever she'd made that mistake in the past, a haunted expression would cross his face, and he'd pull her into a silent embrace, then disappear into his study for hours on end. Seeing her usually cheerful father retreat into a world of pain was worse than not knowing. For now at least, the details of her mother's life would have to remain a mystery.

And so she'd thrown herself headfirst into the world of books. Life was full of mysteries, she quickly discovered—her mother's identity was just one in an infinite list. The difference was, if she wanted to find out why the Egyptians worshiped cats or what sparked the Russian revolution or who was the most powerful female politician of all time, she could always find the answer in a book, if she looked hard enough.

Beatrice gazed into her mom's hazel eyes, flecked with gold like the surface of a honeycomb. Apart from this sole feature, their coloring couldn't have been more different—Beatrice took after her father. For all Beatrice's ginger frizz and freckled pallor, her mother had possessed sleek, dark tresses and skin like alabaster when the sun shone on it. But beneath these obvious traits, as she grew older, Beatrice began to recognize her own image reflected back in the bones of her mother's face and the shape of her features.

She tore her eyes from the photo. She'd come in search of information about a legend, not to ogle her mother's picture for the millionth time. She cast her eyes over the towering bookcase. If there were information to be had, she'd have to find it here, because one thing was conspicuously absent from this study: a computer.

Augustus Archer was staunchly old-school. Although Beatrice had a laptop, her father preferred to use a typewriter for his own work, and in any case, an internet connection was out of the question.

Having grown up—and penned a number of books—long before the digital age, Mr. Archer insisted his daughter do her research the good old-fashioned way: by looking things up in books. He didn't trust the anonymity of the internet. A published book is subject to rigorous fact-checking, and much less likely to have inaccuracies, he maintained. So when all of her schoolmates were writing their essays with the help of Wikipedia and Google, Beatrice was scrounging around the public library or trying her luck with her father's book collection. She grumbled about this, but didn't actually mind. She found comfort in the solidity of an old hard-covered book, in the mathematical reliability of a thorough index. As she cracked open a library tome, she often wondered how many other inquisitive eyes had scanned its pages for answers to their own burning mysteries.

She glanced over the titles on the shelves, which were, not surprisingly, in order of subject. For once she was grateful for her dad's persnickety habits. It wasn't long before she had to drag in a dining room chair to reach the top shelves. At last she spotted a line of books about Rome. There were dozens of them: books on the emperors, the popes, mythology, Renaissance sculpture, Baroque architecture, medieval churches, archaeology . . .

She dove into a book on architecture, turning immediately to the index. In no time, she found a list of fountains. There were at least fifty, but they were all in Italian. She couldn't make sense of a single word. She growled, fighting the urge to throw the book across the room.

Instead, she hopped back up on the chair and pulled down a hefty Italian/English dictionary. "Turtle, turtle, turtle . . . ," she mumbled, thumbing through the back of the English section. "Aha! Turtle: *tartaruga*." She turned back to the index of the architecture book. "Let's see . . . Fontana delle Tartarughe, page 318. That has to be it!"

She located the page and found a photo of the fountain but only one measly paragraph of information.

The Fontana delle Tartarughe, located in the Jewish Ghetto, was designed by Giacomo della Porta and completed in 1588. It was restored in 1658, when four bronze turtles were added by the great Baroque sculptor, Gian Lorenzo Bernini.

Beatrice jotted down the basic facts in her notebook, but skimmed over the last few lines when she saw no mention of the legend. She marked the page with a slip of paper and went on to the next book. When it turned up nothing, she went on to the next, and the next after that.

After a few tedious hours of searching, she was no closer to uncovering the elusive legend. Had Ginevra made it up? But why would she do that?

She closed the last volume with a heavy sigh. After replacing each book, she shuffled back to her room. She leaned on the windowsill and watched the fountain spurting happily, the bronze boys teasing her with their smiles. The slanting rays of afternoon sun turned the neighboring buildings the color of rich, buttery toffee and the fountain threw unexpected shadows over the cobblestones. Beatrice felt the urge to pick up a pencil and re-create it herself.

Her father had encouraged her to try her hand at drawing, especially with all the works of art in Rome for inspiration. She didn't think she'd be any good, but he kept bugging her to give it a chance. She eyed her pristine sketchbook and new set of pencils, sitting unused on a shelf. Why not? She had nothing better to do. She slipped her guidebook and dictionary into her backpack along with the sketching supplies. She wasn't going to be ill prepared this time—she'd learned that lesson the hard way.

Instinctively reaching for her phone, she remembered her little mishap with a rumble in her gut. She fingered the remnants of her phone that lay scattered on her nightstand. It was beyond repair. She wasn't supposed to leave home without it, but surely sitting in the piazza right outside couldn't hurt. She shoved the pieces of broken plastic into the back of a drawer. She'd tell her dad what had happened . . . when and if he asked.

As she stepped into the sunbathed piazza, her mood lifted. The square was buzzing with life. A family speaking what sounded like German consulted a guidebook and an enormous map. A blond girl wearing a wide-brimmed red hat posed in front of the fountain while her boyfriend snapped her picture. A man in a white apron chalked up the day's menu on a blackboard that hung outside a trattoria.

Beatrice settled herself on a shaded bench, dug out her supplies, and got to work. It wasn't easy making her untrained hand follow the curving lines of the fountain, and she used her eraser more than her pencils. Half an hour later, her timid squiggles finally began to resemble something other than a shapeless blob.

She started on the turtles next. Studying their position, she was surprised to notice that they barely touched the rim of the basin. They had to be attached somehow, but they seemed to hover in midair, their hind claws dangling precariously over the edge.

"*Non è niente male*,"[1] came an amused voice over her shoulder.

Beatrice whipped around.

A boy with a mop of brown curls stood behind her, grinning widely as he appraised her work. She flipped the sketchbook shut as bloodred stains streaked across her cheeks.

· ·

1. "Not half bad."

"*Ti conosco, vero?*"[2] he asked with a smile. He had a warm, open face punctuated with dimples, and eyes the color of hot cocoa.

Beatrice's blush deepened as she recognized him. "Um, I . . ."

"Ah," he said, switching into English, "you're the American girl who just moved here, right? You're friends with Alex?" He spoke without a trace of accent.

"Well, n-not exactly," she stammered. "I mean, yes, I'm American, but I'm not friends with Alex. I mean, I just met him the other day . . . the same day I met you. . . ." She was blabbering like an idiot. Apparently she couldn't even speak English anymore. She tried again. "I'm Beatrice." She stood up and held out her free hand.

"Marco. *Piacere*," he said as they shook.

"You speak perfect English—are you Italian or American?"

"I'm half-and-half, actually. Mom's American and Dad's Italian. But I've lived in Rome all my life."

"It must be nice to speak two languages fluently."

"Yeah, it's cool, I guess." Marco glanced at her

. . . .

2. "I know you, right?"

sketchbook with a wry smile. "So you're an artist, eh?"

She couldn't tell if he was serious or looking for a way to poke fun at her.

"Hardly!" she scoffed, hugging the sketchbook to her chest. "I'm just obsessed with this fountain, that's all."

"Me too." He looked up at it. "It's my favorite in the city."

An idea flashed into her head. "Wait. You said you've lived in Rome all your life?"

"Just around the corner."

"Have you ever heard about a legend behind this fountain?"

Marco frowned and lifted his eyebrows. A strange monosyllable issued from his lips. *"Boh!"* It sounded like the croak of a giant toad.

"Excuse me?"

"Sorry, I forgot you're not from Rome." He grinned sheepishly. "That's what we say for *I don't know*."

"Ooo-kay," said Beatrice, furrowing her brow. "Well, I heard there's a legend that this fountain was built in a single night."

"A single night?"

"I know," admitted Beatrice, "it sounds impossible,

but still, I'd like to find out more. You know," she added casually, "just out of curiosity."

"Well, *I've* never heard about that"—he shrugged—"but if anyone has, it'd be my dad. He owns an antique shop just down the street and he's always droning on about neighborhood history. Give him an audience and he'll talk himself hoarse."

"Really?" Beatrice's heart leaped. "Could *I* talk to him?"

"Sure." Marco chuckled. "But if he chews your ear off, don't say I didn't warn you."

seven

ILLUMINATION IN A
DARK SHOP

"La leggenda della Fontana delle Tartarughe?[1] Of course
I know it."

Samuele Morello's voice was a rich, deep bari-
tone. Every word he spoke resounded in his chest
like a vibrating cello string. He sat behind a worktable spread with instruments: a magnifying glass
with a mother-of-pearl handle, a set of minuscule
pliers, a bit of ancient-looking metal he was polish-
ing with a rag.

....

1.   "The Legend of Turtle Fountain?"

The only light came from a lamp hanging a few feet above the worktable, illuminating Signor Morello's face like a spotlight. The rest of the shop was steeped in shadows, though here and there Beatrice spied various artifacts: a fragment of a painted plate depicting a couple embracing, a rusted sword with a dog carved into its hilt, a gold necklace set with amber beads.

Her imagination took wing, inventing histories for each of the inanimate objects—every one a key that opened the door to the past. She saw a wedding banquet with a shy bride and groom eating from the same plate, a young knight taking the image of his beloved dog with him into his first battle, an adolescent girl inheriting a precious necklace on the death of her mother. The scenes flashed before her eyes in the space of a moment, but in that moment she was in a world of her own, a world where time travel was as effortless as daydreaming.

She stepped into a bar of dusty sunlight and was momentarily blinded. The streak of light illuminated a map on the wall and Beatrice couldn't stop her eyes from taking a greedy peek. Hand-drawn lines in cobalt ink outlined what looked like a medieval village surrounded by a wall with a maze of streets twisting higgledy-piggledy.

"A fellow map lover, I see," Signor Morello said with an appraising nod, his voice shaded by a whisper of an accent. "That map shows the Ghetto as it was in the sixteenth century, surrounded by walls and little more than a shantytown. But you came here to learn about a legend, no?"

"Yes!" Beatrice exclaimed, recalling her mission. "I've looked through dozens of books, but I can't find any mention of it."

"Certainly not. Local legends like these are never found in books. They're passed down orally, from generation to generation."

"Really. You never told *me*, Papà," said Marco with a mildly accusatory tone.

"I'm telling you now." He turned his dark, heavy eyes back to Beatrice and nodded to a wooden chair that looked as old as some of the artifacts in the shop. Beatrice sat gingerly as Marco leaned on the corner of his father's worktable. "Tell me, *signorina*, what is the name of the piazza in which the Turtle Fountain is found?"

"Piazza Mattei."

"*Esattamente!*[2] The square was named after the Mattei family, the richest and most powerful family in this neighborhood, since medieval times. Their palace still sits in that very piazza.

"Now," he said, leaning back in his chair, and resting his hands on his ample belly, "according to the legend, sometime at the end of the sixteenth century, a young duke of that family, Muzio Mattei by name, had a weakness for gambling. Muzio was engaged to a beautiful young noblewoman. One evening, shortly before the wedding was to take place, the father of his bride-to-be took Muzio out for a night of cards. The young duke began a dreadful losing streak. By the end of the night, he had lost everything he owned to his future father-in-law, everything, that is, except his ancestral palace, Palazzo Giacomo Mattei."

Signor Morello was a born storyteller. The irresistible pull of his voice drew Beatrice in like the moon pulls at the tide. "The bride's father, not about to wed his daughter to a penniless gambler, announced that the wedding was off. Not willing to lose all of his property *and* his bride, Muzio made one final attempt

. . . .

2. "Exactly!"

54

to salvage his fortune. He wagered his only remaining possession, the family palace, against what he had already lost—including his bride—on an impossible feat: that he could build a fountain in front of his palace in a *single night*."

Beatrice drew in her breath.

"Certain it was a ridiculous bluff," said Signor Morello, "the bride's father accepted the bet. How could he have known that the fountain had already been built and was sitting in a courtyard of the palace, waiting to be assembled? Even the water pipes had been laid under the cobblestones!

"Muzio invited the unsuspecting nobleman to dine at his palace that night, and during the long feast, technicians were hurriedly assembling the fountain. Just as dawn was breaking, the duke threw open the dining room windows to reveal the fountain, exclaiming, 'See what a Mattei can do—even penniless!'"

Signor Morello's dramatic final words reverberated through the shop, and Beatrice had the urge to applaud, as if he'd just delivered Hamlet's most famous soliloquy. Despite Marco's deliberately casual pose, she could tell he was as captivated as she was.

"So did he get his bride back?" Beatrice couldn't resist asking.

"It would appear so. He didn't lose the palace, anyway. At least not yet," he added to himself, smiling as if at a private joke.

Beatrice's insides fluttered but her rational side told her that legends couldn't always be trusted. Not sure she wanted to hear the answer, she asked, "Is it a true story? I mean, do you think it actually happened?" She desperately wanted the legend to be real. She loved fact more than fiction. History, rather than make-believe.

"Ah, *figliola mia*,[3] who can tell?"

"It sounds pretty far-fetched to me," Marco pronounced.

"You'll have to forgive my son; he's a hopeless skeptic. He believes nothing he hears and only half of what he sees." After a thoughtful pause, he continued. "It is true, legends are sometimes merely that: myth. Charming stories invented to explain unusual circumstances."

Beatrice's excitement deflated.

"On the other hand," he said, gazing at her from

. . . .

3.   "my dear girl"

under heavy lids, "these stories had to come from *somewhere*. Every legend has some nugget of truth."

A tingle ran down Beatrice's spine and she shot Marco an exultant look, her mind alight with the flame of possibility.

For the rest of the day, she could think of nothing else. Over dinner, she recounted the legend to her father, and later, in her bedroom, she could barely concentrate on her Italian homework. The words *Muzio* and *Mattei* and *tartarughe* swam on the blank page in front of her. As she scrubbed the day's grime from her freckled face, she repeated the legend over and over in her head until the words and images had seeped into her skin, her blood, the very marrow of her bones, and, eventually, her dreams.

eight

A MAN IN BLACK AND A
REAPPEARING ACT

Clang!

Beatrice awoke with a start.

She had dreamed she'd fallen into the Turtle Fountain. She was riding on the back of one of the dolphins, chasing the bronze boys through cascades and torrents. Duke Muzio had gambled away his fortune again, and the fountain was being destroyed. It was being hacked to pieces!

Clang!

Beatrice sat bolt upright, her heart thumping. It was just a crazy dream. Still, she couldn't shake the feeling something was amiss. She listened intently but couldn't hear a thing, not the *vroom* of passing scooters or the laughter of people wandering through the square.

Clang!

The sound from her dream. Was she imagining it? Her head was still foggy with sleep. Either that or she was still dreaming.

Clang!

She slid out of bed and crept through the dark room. Hidden from view behind the shutters, she peered down onto the piazza below.

Her eyes widened. The square was dimly lit, but there was no mistaking what she saw. A man dressed in black from head to foot—his face hidden under a ski mask—perched on the fountain's edge. He held an unwieldy object under his left arm, and in his right hand a crowbar.

For a moment Beatrice stood frozen, her mind unable to process what she was seeing. It wasn't until the man hopped down, his sneakers hitting the cobblestones with a *squish*, that Beatrice snapped back to reality. A gush of horror flooded her as she realized that instead of four, just one bronze turtle sat atop the fountain. She now recognized the object tucked under the man's arm: one of the turtles! The other two were nowhere in sight.

The man slipped the turtle into a bag and hurried over to a beat-up red motor scooter parked at the edge of the square. He strapped the bundle onto the back. A moment later he again waded into the fountain, hoisted himself up, and raised his weapon against the last remaining turtle.

Clang!

Beatrice tried to scream, but—like in a dream—her voice stuck in her throat.

The next thing she knew she was racing down the hallway. She hadn't run to her father's room in the middle of the night for years, but this was an emergency.

"Dad, Dad!" she shouted as she ran to his bed.

He sat up instantly. "What is it, Beatrice? What's happened?"

"The turtles! They're being stolen!" she blurted.

"What turtles?"

"I saw someone stealing the turtles off the fountain!"

"What?" He rubbed his eyes.

"I had a dream that the fountain was being destroyed . . . and I heard this terrible clanging noise . . . and when I woke up, there was a man in a mask, stealing the turtles right off it! Dad, he's down there now, we have to do something!"

"Beatrice," he said patiently, suppressing a yawn, "it was just a dream—"

"No, it wasn't! I saw it. It was real."

"Beatrice, sweet pea, go back to bed."

"No, Dad, I'm telling you: I saw the turtles being stolen! Look for yourself!" She gestured to the shuttered windows, but his bedroom was on the opposite side of the building.

"Beatrice . . ." The patience in his voice was wearing thin.

"Please, come look from my room!" Panic rose from her stomach until she could taste it. "You have to believe me!"

With an exasperated sigh, he eased himself out of bed. The time it took him to don his robe and slippers felt like an eternity. With every *tick* of his alarm clock, the turtles slipped farther away.

Beatrice dragged her sleepy father into her bedroom and over to the window. As she pushed open the shutters she dreaded what she'd see.

A single streetlamp cast a murky light on the piazza. There was no sign of the thief or his scooter. The fountain gurgled away as it always did, and perched on top, as if nothing had happened, were four bronze turtles.

"But . . . ," she sputtered.

"Beatrice!" Her father's patience snapped. "What's gotten into you tonight?"

"I saw it, I swear!" But though she wouldn't have admitted it, doubt was creeping in.

"No more nonsense!" he said sternly. "It was a nightmare, that's all. Go back to bed. We'll talk about this in the morning."

He seldom raised his voice so she knew he'd heard enough. Anything else she said would be pointless. He closed her shutters with a bang and waited as she padded back to bed. Then he leaned down to kiss her forehead. "Try to get some rest now, okay?"

"But I . . . ," Beatrice mumbled uselessly.

"Good night," he said with finality and closed the door behind him.

As she lay in the dark, images spun round and round her mind: the turtles, the man in black, the red scooter. She *couldn't* have just dreamed it all. She'd seen it. . . . She *knew* she'd seen it happen. . . .

Or had she?

She should have been relieved the fountain was undamaged, but her mind was a haze of confusion and doubt. She was about to pull the covers over her head, but a thought wouldn't stop poking at her brain: *It didn't feel like a dream.*

Unable to resist just one more look, she tore out of bed, strode to the window, and peeked through the shutters. There they were: four undeniably solid turtles. Had she imagined the whole thing? Would she have to doubt her sanity now, along with everything else?

Then she noticed something small and black, floating in the lowest basin of the fountain.

Without giving herself time for second thoughts, she donned her bathrobe and flip-flops and tiptoed to the front door. By morning it would be too late; any possible clues might be swept away. She had to investigate *now.*

As she eased back the bolt, she tried not to imagine her father's fury if he found out what she was up to. She held her breath and pulled the door open a crack, exhaling only after she'd soundlessly scampered through. She left the door ajar and crept down the stairs and out into the piazza. Besides the sloshing of the fountain, the night was completely silent. Not a soul was about. And just as she'd noticed from her window, a black object was floating in the water. She reached over the fountain's edge and gingerly fished it out.

A glove! Surely one of the pair the man had been wearing. She knew it: it hadn't been a dream! But that didn't explain why the turtles had suddenly reappeared. Why in the world would someone risk hacking them off, only to put them right back on again?

She wrung out the glove and stuffed it into her bathrobe pocket, then proceeded to search for more clues. She circled the fountain three times, checking every crevice and cranny, every inch of the marble border. Nothing.

A street sweeper rumbled around the corner, making its nightly cleanup trip through the neighborhood. Beatrice hurried back to her building and flew up the stairs, her mind whirring with possibilities. Something odd was going on, but it didn't make a scrap of sense. She was about to ease open her door when she heard a sinister creak behind her.

She whipped around. A shadowy figure lurked in the doorway of the apartment opposite, staring out with shrewd eyes that were lit from within.

Beatrice swallowed hard, silently instructing herself she didn't believe in ghosts. "He-hello?" Her voice quavered.

A tiny dog with fluffy white fur poked its head between the apparition's slippered feet, growling like an angry powder puff. Beatrice's eyes traveled back up the length of the figure to find a woman's halo of hair, just as white as her dog's. She sighed with relief. It wasn't a ghost—just her next-door neighbor. "I hope I didn't disturb you, ma'am," she whispered.

"*Buonanotte, signorina,*"[1] said the old woman with an unreadable gleam in her eye. Then the door creaked shut.

---

1. "Goodnight, miss."

nine

THE BERNINI CONNECTION

The next morning, Beatrice could barely concentrate on her Italian lesson. She was tempted to tell her teacher what she'd witnessed, to confide in *someone*. But she resisted—what if Ginevra didn't believe her? How embarrassing if, like her father, her tutor thought she was making it all up.

When at last the lesson was over, she raced back to her room and locked the door. Now, where had she left her nighttime discovery? She eyed her bathrobe with a bubble of excitement in her belly. Snatching it up, she noticed the entire pocket was damp from where the wet glove had spent the night. She pulled it out by one of its soggy fingertips.

What had seemed like such a thrilling clue last night was, in the harsh light of day, just a smelly old glove. A glove that proved nothing. Who would believe her story about a turtle thief when the turtles were *still there*, sitting atop the fountain for all to see? She barely believed herself.

Standing there with a wet glove in her hand, she suddenly felt like a silly little girl. What made her think *she'd* be able to figure out what had happened?

And what had really happened anyway? There was probably a perfectly logical explanation. Maybe the man she saw was a city maintenance worker, taking the turtles down to be cleaned. The idea that there might be some mystery behind what she witnessed was childish and far-fetched. Time to grow up and stop imagining things, she chided herself, flinging the glove into the trash.

Still, questions kept niggling at her brain: if the man was simply cleaning the fountain, why in the middle of the night? And why would he wear a mask? And what about the glove? Someone on authorized business wouldn't have been in such a hurry that he'd drop his glove and not have time to retrieve it.

Drawn to the window by an invisible force, Beatrice gazed down at the turtles as if they might come to life and tell her what had happened. As always, their bronze shells glinted in the late July sun, but something wasn't right. She squinted down at them; something about their position seemed off.

She dug out her half-finished sketch, remembering how the turtles had seemed to balance half-suspended on the edge of the basin. Unwilling to rely on either her memory or her amateur drawing, she opened her guidebook to a photo of the fountain.

She grabbed her binoculars and studied the turtles through the tiny lenses, comparing them to the ones in the photograph. Was it her imagination, or did they now rest on the brim more securely? She'd have to get a closer look.

Outside, humidity hung heavy in the air, making Beatrice's clothes stick to her skin and her hair frizz out like a great burning bush. She smoothed it down distractedly as she approached the fountain. Circling slowly, she scrutinized each turtle in turn, all the while consulting the photo in the guidebook.

It was barely perceptible—she'd probably never have noticed if she hadn't been sketching them the day before—but the turtles *had* been moved. Why someone would risk pulling them off just to change their position she couldn't fathom. But there was no longer any doubt: the turtles had been tampered with.

Could it have been some elaborate prank? An attempted robbery gone wrong?

She sat on a bench and closed her eyes. She replayed exactly what she'd witnessed the night before, reconstructing the scene behind her eyelids. She followed the movements of the man in black with her mind's eye as he teetered on the edge of the fountain, the ungainly turtle under his arm.

Curiously, her mind lingered on a trivial detail: the soggy *squish* of his sneakers as they hit the cobblestones. Why did that ordinary sound seem so oddly significant? A reedy voice interrupted her thoughts.

"Buongiorno, signorina."

Beatrice's eyes flew open. An elderly woman stood at her side, dressed in a neat maroon suit, her white hair coiffed to perfection. If it hadn't been for the small white dog beside her, Beatrice would never have recognized her as the ghostly figure she'd encountered the night before.

"Buongiorno, signora," she said politely. *"Io mi chiamo*

Beatrice." At this real-life use of her newly acquired Italian skills, a gush of pride pooled in her belly.

"*Piacere.* I am Mirella Costaguti," said the old lady imperiously in subtly accented English. "It appears we are neighbors."

Beatrice blushed. It must have seemed pretty odd for a thirteen-year-old girl to be out and about in a bathrobe in the middle of the night. Would Signora Costaguti say something to Beatrice's father?

As Beatrice tried to come up with a plausible explanation for her nighttime wanderings, Signora Costaguti observed, "You seem quite taken with this fountain."

"Yes," Beatrice breathed, "I love it, especially . . . especially the turtles," she added, half to herself.

"You have a good eye. Della Porta was an excellent fountain designer, but Bernini was a *genius.*"

"Bernini?" The name sounded vaguely familiar but she couldn't place it.

"Gian Lorenzo Bernini, the sculptor, of course." She looked appalled that Beatrice didn't know of him. "He is one of the greatest artists of the Baroque period, one of the greatest artists of all time! His artistic expression, his creativity, his technical ability, they are virtually unrivaled. The *Apollo and Daphne*, the

Fountain of the Four Rivers, so many masterpieces—
all priceless."

"Bernini made *these* turtles?"

"That is correct. They were not part of Della Porta's
original design, but added by Bernini almost a century
later, when the fountain was restored."

Something clicked inside Beatrice's mind, like a
key turning in a lock. It all made sense. The turtles
were not just adorable—they were the work of one of
the most important sculptors in history. Sculptures by
such a famous artist, even small ones, must be worth a
fortune. No wonder someone was trying to steal them!
And if they had failed the first time, they'd definitely
try again.

"Well, it was a pleasure to meet you, *cara*," Signora
Costaguti said stiffly, "but I'm afraid I must be going."

"Um, you—you won't mention to my father . . . ,"
Beatrice faltered ". . . about last night?"

"Last night? Whatever do you mean?" Signora
Costaguti's face was blank, but a knowing spark shone
in her eye. "*Andiamo, Artemisia,*"[1] she cooed to her
dog, and they disappeared down a narrow street.

. . . .

1. "Let's go, Artemisia"

ten

AN UNLIKELY ALLY

Beatrice circled the fountain, reveling in her secret knowledge. How many people looked at this fountain every
day? She alone knew it had been tampered with. And
now she knew why: the turtles were worth a fortune.

As she digested this new piece of information, her
eyes roamed the square. They hovered on the palazzo
opposite her building, the white one with the walled-
up window, the window that had given her such a
fright her first night in Rome.

Her first night in Rome . . . *That's* where she'd
heard that squishing sound! In a flash it came back to
her. She'd completely forgotten about the man she'd

seen lurking in the piazza on her first jet-lagged night in Rome. His sneakers had made a *squish-squish* noise, just like those of the masked man last night. Such an ordinary noise, it could have been made by any number of sneakers—it didn't mean a thing by itself. But the man she'd seen from her window that first night had been tall and lanky, just like the one who'd attacked the fountain.

She closed her eyes, trying to recall exactly what that shifty young man with the backpack had looked like, but all she could remember was a shaved head, a long-limbed body, and snakelike tattoos running up and down his arms.

It wasn't much to go on. Still, her instincts told her the two men were one and the same. But even if she was right, what did it prove?

She sighed with frustration and stared at the false window. What was the point of walling up a window? And why would anyone have wanted to block a view of the Turtle Fountain?

She wandered over to investigate. Carved above the palace's monumental wooden doors was a marble coat of arms featuring a checkerboard pattern with a diagonal slash running across it. Inscribed above were three astonishing words: *Palazzo Giacomo Mattei.*

So this was Duke Mattei's palace! According to the legend, the duke built the Turtle Fountain in order to win back his property and his bride—and he had succeeded. Why then had someone, presumably of the same family, walled up a window that looked out onto it?

Nailed to the front door was a notice. Beatrice stomped her feet in frustration that she couldn't read it; then she heard her father's voice—*if you give up every time you meet with a challenge, you'll never get anywhere.* She remembered the pocket dictionary in her bag. She fished it out and began to look up the words.

She started with the bolded line across the top: *Avviso di Asta Pubblica.*

Avviso: notice.

di: of (she knew that already from her lessons).

Asta: auction.

Pubblica: public (obviously).

A public auction! Here in this very palace! She scanned the notice to find out when. There it was, at the bottom of the page: *Esposizione: martedì il 27 luglio dalle ore 15.00 alle ore 19.00. Asta: domenica l'1 agosto alle ore 17.00.* She gleefully translated the dates and times in her head: Tuesday, July 27 (today!) from three to seven p.m., and Sunday, August 1 at five p.m.

The auction was her in. If she could just get inside the palace, maybe she could find out more about the legend. She knew that somehow the legend was connected to whatever had happened to the turtles. It had to be. She felt it in her gut.

She glanced at her watch: two-thirty. She had a half hour. The only appropriate thing to do to fill the time would be to get a gelato, Italy's version of ice cream—that was *way* better than ice cream.

As she made her way down the bending streets to her favorite *gelateria*, she put the legend and the fountain and the turtles and the man in black and the walled-up window and all the rest of it out of her head, and focused instead on which flavor to get.

Chocolate, of course, was excellent—but it was too hot for chocolate. Perhaps something fruity like melon or peach. Lemon was refreshing, but a bit sour. Maybe they had mango. . . .

She skipped into the *gelateria* with the taste of a dozen fruits on her lips. But before she could try out her limited vocabulary with the shop assistant, she recognized someone. A young man with floppy brown hair was tucking into a strawberry gelato armed with a tiny plastic spoon. It was the snooty tour guide who'd mocked her the week before.

First she tried to avoid him, still burning with embarrassment at how she'd humiliated herself in front of all those people. Then she had a brilliant thought: why not ask *him* about the legend? He was a tour guide; who better to know random bits of information?

Forgoing her gelato (and a good deal of pride), Beatrice gathered her courage and walked up to him just as he was downing the last of his ice cream. "Excuse me?"

He turned and looked at her, his eyelids drooping as if her existence bored him beyond words.

"Excuse me," she repeated with her most winning smile. "You're a tour guide, aren't you? I was hoping you could answer a question." She prayed he wouldn't recognize her.

"Ah, you again!" he exclaimed in his cut-glass British accent. "Been to *the Colosseum* lately?" he sneered, glancing in the direction of the Theater of Marcellus.

Beatrice bristled. "Yes, well, um, I was wondering if you knew anything about the legend of the Turtle Fountain?"

"Ah, *la Fontana delle Tartarughe . . .*," he crooned, over-enunciating each word. "The loveliest fountain in Rome."

"Oh, you think so too?" Maybe he wasn't so bad after all.

"I'd love to answer your questions, but I have a tour. . . ."

"Please, just a minute of your time! You see . . ." She thought up an excuse quickly. "I have to write a school paper on it, and I've looked through a dozen books but I just can't find the last bit of information—"

"A school paper? In July?" He raised a dubious eyebrow.

"It's for summer school," she gabbled. "But, you know, it's fine. If you don't know anything about it, I suppose I could . . ."

Just as she'd hoped, he took the bait.

"Oh, believe me, I know *all* about that fountain. I practically wrote my dissertation on it."

Dissertation, smishertation. I bet you don't know the turtles were ripped off it last night, she wanted to shout.

But she held her tongue. Instead she said, "It's all right. I'm sure you're very busy, and the last thing I want to do is waste your time—"

"Please. What do you want to know?" he said studying his fingernails with a sniff. "You have been fortunate enough to locate an expert."

"I know about the legend of the Mattei duke who had the fountain built in one night to win back his property and his bride. But what I can't figure out is why one of the windows of his palace was walled-up and painted over. Does it have anything to do with the legend?" She took a deep breath. She'd spewed it out as quickly as possible so he wouldn't have a chance to interrupt. She looked up at him expectantly.

He said nothing, just stood there and smiled, enjoying her anticipation.

"Yes, *that window*." He grinned to himself, as if deliberately leaving her out of an inside joke.

"Does it have anything to do with the legend?" she persisted.

"It has *everything* to do with it," he said dramatically. "The duke won his property back, and his bride; *everyone* knows *that* story. But what most people *don't* know is that the bride wasn't so happy to be won.

Some say she was in love with someone else; some say she was simply terrified of the duke's infamous cruelty. Either way, she was being forced to marry him because his family was so wealthy and powerful. She begged her father to call it off, but the marriage contract had already been signed and he couldn't back out without drastic social and financial consequences. Not even his ploy to get the duke to gamble away his fortune worked. When he lost the bet about the fountain, his daughter's fate was sealed."

Beatrice gasped. The picture of the duke and his bride that she held in her mind shifted like sand. Now instead of a love that couldn't be broken, she saw a portrait of malice and fear.

"Inevitably, the marriage turned out to be an unhappy one. The young duchess ordered the window through which her father had first seen the fountain to be boarded up forever."

"Then it's not just a legend!" Beatrice blurted. "It all really happened!"

"This is a country that loves stories." He shrugged. "Maybe it did; maybe it didn't. Who are we to say?"

Beatrice wanted to ask him a dozen more questions, but he was gathering his things and glancing pointedly at his watch. "Thank you so much . . ."

"Nigel. Nigel Dundersnitch," he said with a flick of his hair.

Beatrice suppressed a giggle at the unfortunate moniker.

"I'm Beatrice, by the way. Beatrice Archer. I can't tell you how much I appreciate your help."

Nigel's eyes narrowed. "Why are you so interested in this obscure bit of history anyway?"

"Um . . ." She racked her brain for a plausible excuse but came up with zilch. "No reason!" she chirped, putting on her most innocent face.

Nigel didn't look convinced. "If I were you, I'd be careful of who I spoke to about this," he said, suddenly serious.

"And why is that?" Beatrice demanded.

"That family," he said, glancing over his shoulder as if to make sure no one was listening, "the Mattei family . . ." He lowered his voice to a whisper and Beatrice had to lean in to hear him. "Legend has it they're *cursed*."

eleven

THE FRENCHMAN

If Nigel had thought his warning would dissuade her from further investigations, well, it had done the exact opposite. She was more convinced than ever that the legend had something to do with the attack on the fountain, and that there was only one logical place to look for answers: the Mattei Palace.

Back in the square, a small crowd had gathered at the palace's front door. She got in line behind a few dozen well-dressed Italians who were gradually being let in by a doorman. When it was finally her turn to enter, the doorman took one look at her shorts, T-shirt, flip-flops, backpack, and lack of adult chaperone, and barked, "*Niente bambini non accompagnati!*"

She stared at him in utter bewilderment.

"No unaccompaneed cheeldren!" he translated gruffly.

"But . . ."

"*Arrivederci.*"

She was unceremoniously pushed out of line, and a snooty middle-aged couple elbowed past and walked inside. So that was it? They weren't going to let her in?

Refusing to accept defeat, she gathered her determination and stomped back to her apartment. "I'll find a way to get into that palace if it's the last thing I do!" she proclaimed aloud.

Back in her bedroom, she ransacked her wardrobe. She settled on a lavender knee-length wraparound skirt and a flowy gray silk blouse. She slipped on a pair of black sandals, pinned up her hair, and squirted on some perfume.

Grabbing a demure handbag, barely big enough for her keys—let alone her cell phone, had it been intact—she appraised herself in the mirror. Not bad. She looked like a completely different girl. Still, it only solved half the problem. Now she looked presentable, but she was still *unaccompanied*.

Could she pass for a few years older? Doubtful; she was short for her age as it was. Then how would she slip past the doorman? She marched out of her apartment. She'd think of something.

The line now snaked around the building. It seemed as though all of Rome's elite had turned up in her little piazza to score some antique bargains. She sidled up to the back of the line, eyeing the people around her. Could one of them help her? How would she even ask in her nonexistent Italian?

Her eyes shifted to an older gentleman standing beside her, humming to himself and reading a newspaper. He was short and rotund, with salt-and-pepper hair and a trim gray beard. His eyes sported clusters of wrinkles on either side, like her dad's—the kind made by a lifetime of smiling. He shuffled the pages of the paper and Beatrice noticed it had English headlines. Before she had time to stop herself, she shrieked, "Are you English?"

The man rolled his eyes at that unpleasant suggestion and replied in a thick accent, "No, I am not English, zank 'eavens, I am French! But I do *speak*

English. 'Ow can I be of service, *ma'moiselle?*" he asked, folding the paper and tucking it under a plump little elbow.

"I . . . um . . ." She racked her brain for an appropriate question. "Do you happen to know . . . if you need an appointment to attend the auction?"

"But tonight is not ze auction, *ma'moiselle.*"

"What? I read the notice on the door. . . . I thought it said Tuesday and Sunday. . . ." What had she misunderstood this time?

"Today is the exposition, for prospective buyers to view ze collection. Ze auction itself is on Sunday."

"Oh. Well, that's okay. I just want to visit the palace."

"Now, why would a leettle child like yourself want to visit zis palace? Certainly zere are more exciting sites in Rome?"

"Um . . ." How many times would she find herself lying to a total stranger today? "I just love the . . . er . . . history of the Mattei family. You know, the fountain, the legend . . ." She eyed the palace entrance, inching closer by the second. If she could just keep him talking, maybe the doorman would think they were together and let her in.

"*Ah, oui.*" He gazed at the fountain and sighed. "Certainly ze most beautifool fountain in Rome." His eyes glinted as he looked at the turtles, as if they held the answer to a riddle.

"It's my favorite too." Beatrice struggled to keep her voice steady.

"You know, of course, zat ze Mattei family is completely impoverished."

"Impoverished?"

"Zey're out of money!" He cackled with glee. "Ze old *duc* from way back when wasn't ze only one wiz a gambling problem. His descendants 'ave lost everyzing. Why do you zink zey're 'aving zis auction? Zeir debts are enormous, and ze sale of ze palace won't be enough; zey're selling off *all* zeir possessions."

Beatrice hadn't stopped to wonder *why* there was an auction taking place. She'd only seen it as a way to get inside. She hadn't imagined the Mattei family might still *live there* after all these years.

"A family zat was once so rich and powerfool, since ze Middle Ages. 'Alf a century of dominance in zis neighborhood! And now zey are *ruined*."

"How did it happen?" Beatrice asked tentatively.

"Zey are cursed!" he shouted dramatically. "It is ze

only explanation. Zey owned four palaces in zis neighborhood alone, and others around ze city. One by one, zey lost zem all. Zis is ze only one left. It belongs to ze heir of ze last remaining branch of ze family, and by Sunday, it too will be sold, and zat will be ze nail in ze coffin of ze 'ouse of Mattei."

"Who would have wanted to curse them?" Beatrice wondered aloud.

The Frenchman looked sinister. "In zose days, *ma chère*, all powerful families 'ad enemies. Ze Mattei more zan most."

The Frenchman's revelations were so fascinating that Beatrice didn't notice they had reached the front of the line. The doorman narrowed his eyes at her, and just when she was convinced he was going to throw her out of line again, he seemed to change his mind, and waved them both in with a bored shrug.

They walked through the immense doorway into a cobbled courtyard. A sweeping staircase led to a covered balcony framed with columns and arches, a loggia she'd read it was called. She marveled at the size of the doors and the Frenchman explained that in a Renaissance palace, the doorway had to be big enough to allow horse-drawn carriages to pass through to the courtyard, which would be fitted with a carriage house and stables. There were no living quarters on the ground floor, just the service facilities, kitchen, pantry, and the like. All the most important rooms, where the family entertained, were one floor up, on the piano nobile, the noble floor.

Once inside, they followed dozens of eager visitors up another grand staircase to the piano nobile to view the items up for sale. Despite her gratitude to this old man for the information he'd divulged, now that she was inside, she was itching to explore, *alone*.

"It was so nice to meet you, Mr. . . ."

"Likewise, *ma'moiselle*! Enjoy your visit!" he said with a jovial wink, and disappeared into the crowd.

twelve

A DUCHESS AND HER DIARY

Beatrice stood at the top of the staircase, her eyes widening with wonder. Opulence overwhelmed every corner of her vision: antique cabinets, porcelain statuettes, gilded mirrors, silver candlesticks taller than she was, marble-topped tables, alabaster vases, tapestries, sculptures, busts, and row upon row of gilt-framed paintings, all with a backdrop of paneled walls and frescoed ceilings.

Discreet placards described (in English as well as Italian, she noticed gratefully) the articles on display with opening bid prices. And the prices were astronomical! She'd forgotten for a moment that she was in an auction showroom, not a museum.

As she meandered down a corridor hung with large oil paintings, she noticed the suspicious eyes of a guard following her every step. *Don't panic*, she told herself, and quietly latched onto a nearby group of adults who were too absorbed with the art to notice her. Lagging behind them, she passed one enormous landscape painting after another, but she was growing antsy. She hadn't come here to admire the collection; she'd come to gather information.

Where to begin? The palace was dripping with stuff. Expensive stuff, but stuff nonetheless. She didn't even know what she was looking for.

Around the corner was another painting gallery, this one full of portraits. Stern and imposing men. Rich ladies, dripping with jewels. Opulently dressed children, posing like miniature adults.

Beatrice's pace slackened in front of a small, dark painting. Under a layer of soot, a young woman gazed out with a sorrowful expression. As Beatrice approached the portrait, a gust of air blew in from the windows, setting the chandeliers clinking and rainbow bursts dancing on the walls. The chatter of the visitors faded into the background, replaced by a faint hum that hung in the air like a distant swarm of bees. Time lagged behind its usual relentless pace and Beatrice's breathing—even her blinking—slowed.

As her probing eyes met the painted lady's mournful ones, invisible pins pricked at her arms and legs. Unlike the idealized appearance of some of the other portraits, this one looked startlingly real. Beatrice had the chilling sensation that she was looking at an actual woman, not a painted one.

The lady in the portrait was dressed in a simple gown of green satin and velvet, a gold braided sash tied around her waist. Her dark, lustrous hair framed her slender face, and an amber-colored stole hung loosely around her shoulders. She sat rigidly on a high-backed chair, a small leather book clasped in her hand.

The background was dull and dark. The only light came from a tiny window in the corner of the canvas, creating harsh shadows that made the painting look . . . sinister. Despite the canvas's thick layer of grime, the woman's melancholy gaze shone through like a plea for help. What could this beautiful, wealthy lady have been so sad about? Beatrice glanced at the placard near the corner of the frame.

Portrait of a duchess of the Mattei family, circa 1600, artist unknown.

Beatrice's eyes widened. *Duchess. Mattei. 1600?*

She trembled as she calculated the dates in her head. The Turtle Fountain was built in 1588, so Muzio Mattei must have gotten married shortly thereafter. His bride would, naturally, have become a duchess, and would probably have been alive twelve years later when this portrait was painted. Could it be . . . *her?*

That would explain why she looked so sad; according to Nigel, she was forced to marry a man she didn't love. Beatrice's insides squirmed. Putting a face to the legend made it suddenly, startlingly real.

She scrutinized the painting for more clues. The woman's eyes were tinged with red, as if she'd been crying, and her fingertips were stained with ink. On the spine of the leather book, a few letters were faintly etched in gold: *C-A-T-E* . . . her fingers hid the rest.

Despite her urge to keep exploring, Beatrice was reluctant to abandon the painting. She felt inexplicably linked to this lady with the melancholy eyes. But as intriguing as the painting was, it didn't give her any answers. She tore herself away and wandered into yet another sumptuous showroom.

Along the right wall, a beefy man in a too-tight suit stood with his back against a set of closed doors, his arms crossed over his chest like a Russian dancer. Whatever was behind *those* doors was sure to be interesting, Beatrice speculated. But the man's hardened expression and beady-eyed glare made it painfully clear that whatever he was guarding was not on display to mere auctiongoers like her.

Beatrice hurried toward the next showroom before she attracted any more attention. Just as she was about to turn the corner, the double doors behind her burst open with a loud *clack*. She peeked over her shoulder. A man came out, this one tall and slender with thinning dark hair and a beak-like nose. He slammed the door behind him, snapped a few short words at the barrel-chested guard, and the two men disappeared down the corridor in the opposite direction.

Beatrice stood stalk-still. Whether through a simple act of negligence or by the hand of fate, the men had left the door unlocked. Her eyes darted from right to left. The chattering visitors were absorbed in the objects on display and no one glanced her way. She stealthily approached the door and placed her hand on the knob, when a thought occurred to her: what if someone was still inside? She shrugged. Then she'd just pretend she was lost. She'd never solve anything without taking a few risks. She cast a surreptitious glance around and cracked open the door. With a fortifying breath, she slithered inside.

Empty. No sooner had she let out a sigh of relief than her eyes widened with wonder. Innumerable books climbed the walls like the branches of an exotic creeping plant. Row after row of leather-bound volumes filled nearly every inch of wall space, reaching all the way to the gilded ceiling. A person could spend their entire life in a library like this and never scratch the surface. It made her father's library back in Boston seem downright puny by comparison.

Pausing in her marveling, Beatrice suddenly remembered her mission. Right. She was there to search for clues, not drool over a stranger's book collection. Unfortunately, she had no idea what she was looking for. She tried to tap into her intuition, which had been spot-on so far: it'd led her to the Frenchman, and the duchess's portrait. All she had to do was keep following her gut, and if there were anything to find, she'd find it.

At least that's what she kept telling herself. In reality, the seconds ticked by faster and faster—the sinister-looking men could reappear at any moment. Her belly dropped like a yo-yo at the thought. If there was a clue in here, she needed to find it soon.

She raked her eyes over the contents of the room. There were too many books—and probably all in Italian. Starting there was not an option. A massive antique globe occupied one corner, and wine-colored leather sofas and armchairs crouched here and there. A broad mahogany desk seemed like the most likely place to start.

On one corner sat an old-fashioned fountain pen, a glass inkwell, and a blotter. Did these people live in the past or did they just act like they did? Several papers were scattered across the desktop. The first one looked like a building floor plan, but not any building she'd ever seen. The plan was shaped like a giant half-moon dissected by angled lines, with random squiggles drawn on in pencil. The next two papers were letters scrawled in what looked like Italian. The rest of the documents were equally bewildering.

She sighed. She was getting nowhere. Maybe her instinct had been wrong. Maybe the clue to solving this puzzle wasn't in the palace after all. Was she in over her head?

And yet, she alone knew someone had tried to steal Bernini's turtles. It was her duty to try to find out who, if only to prevent them from succeeding the next time.

She walked resolutely toward the towering shelves. The books were ensconced behind glass doors and the light was so dim she could barely decipher the titles. She tried one of the doors but it was locked fast.

About to stamp her feet in frustration, she noticed a spiral staircase carved of rich dark wood. It led to a narrow landing that snaked around the upper walls of the library, providing access to the books on the highest shelves. The lighting up there was better, and there were no glass cabinets, as far as she could tell. The books were just sitting there, waiting to be picked up by a curious reader. Without a second's hesitation, she bounded up the stairs.

She trawled the narrow landing searching for something, anything that might shed some light on this mystery. The books were stacked tightly together under a thick layer of dust. It looked like they hadn't been touched in a century. She ran a finger along the backs of a random row of books where the light was brightest. She scanned the titles, naively hoping what she needed would magically reveal itself.

Cassiodoro, Flavio Magno
Castel Sant'Angelo
Catechismo della Chiesa Cattolica
Caterina
Catilina, Lucio Sergio
Catone, Marco Porcio

Beatrice froze. She worked her way back a few titles, stopping when her finger hovered over a simple brown leather book. The name *Caterina* was engraved in faded gold on the spine. Her mind flitted to the image of the book in the portrait she'd seen earlier, the letters *C-A-T-E* etched in an identical manner. Her hand trembled as she eased it out.

It was unmistakable: this was the book from the portrait. The narrow volume had a ridge of dust along the top. She blew it off lightly. Slowly, her heart knocking against her ribs, she eased the book open. The binding creaked. When was the last time human hands had touched it? She tremulously turned one page, then another, and just as she'd imagined—just as she'd hoped—the brittle yellowed pages were filled not with printed text but faded, elegant penmanship.

The penmanship of a noble lady.

A lady called Caterina.

A duchess.

Beatrice squatted down and, balancing the diary on one knee, gingerly turned one page after another. She ran a finger over the pale brown ink, but even if she could have read Italian, the penmanship was so foreign she could barely make out the letters. The dates were easier, and she determined the journal began in May 1592. Exactly right for the diary of the woman for whom the Turtle Fountain had been built.

High on the landing, hunched over the diary, Beatrice lost track of time and place. She turned the musty pages and scanned the unintelligible words that had been scrawled on them all those years ago. Here and there, tiny blots smudged the words; could they be four-hundred-year-old teardrops? Gooseflesh spread across Beatrice's arms as she touched this piece of living, breathing history. She could almost see the hand of the woman in the portrait as it dragged a quill across these very pages.

The clack of the double doors snapped Beatrice back to the present and sent her blood racing through her veins. Someone must have seen her sneak into the library and now the beefy guard was coming for her! He'd find her thumbing through a four-century-old book and throw her out on her ear, maybe even notify her father. She'd never be allowed out of the house again!

She held her breath and slid down as far as she could, but it was no use. Whoever it was knew she was up there, and he was coming for her.

thirteen

A SECRET MEETING AND A RUMOR

"Allora, now we can talk in private," came a deep voice with a faint Italian accent after the door had clicked shut once more.

Beatrice couldn't believe her ears. Whoever it was *wasn't* here to nab her! For the moment, she was safe. All she had to do was stay put and keep quiet, and she could sneak out after they left.

"Excellent," said another man. His voice was accented as well but not with Italian. In fact, the rhythm of it was strikingly familiar.

"Please, make yourself comfortable," said the Italian.

"Zank you very much."

The Frenchman!

Beatrice couldn't resist a tiny peek through the railing of the landing. Sure enough, the friendly old man who'd helped her into the palace was easing himself onto a leather couch. The other man, a white pate showing through his dark hair, was hurriedly stuffing the papers on his desk into a drawer. He slammed it shut and turned a tiny key, which he then slipped into his pocket. When he turned around to reveal the beak-like nose of the man she'd seen earlier, Beatrice had just enough time to duck out of sight, flattening herself onto the floor of the landing. If she moved a muscle or made a sound, she'd be discovered.

"You shouldn't have come here today, Monsieur Cambriolage," said the Beak Nose. "We cannot be seen together. No one must know we are in negotiations. If you wanted to view the collection, I could have arranged a private viewing for you at another time."

"Don't you zink zat would 'ave looked even more suspicious?"

Beatrice tried to follow their conversation over the clamor of her pounding heart.

"Perhaps. Regardless, now that you're here, can you

please tell me what was so important that it couldn't wait for our meeting?"

"My client 'as 'eard a nasty rumor."

"What kind of rumor?"

"Zat you are planning to sell 'im *fakes*."

"Are you insinuating . . ."

"I am not insinuating anyzing, young man," the Frenchman replied with a good-humored chuckle. "I'm *telling* you what our sources told us. If it's not true, zen you have nozzing to worry about."

"It is absolutely untrue, and I resent the implication." He paused, as if searching for the right words. "I can arrange for you to be in a car, at a discreet distance, but still within view when the articles are . . . removed. You can follow the transport vehicle directly to the drop-off point. Will that satisfy you?"

"Very much so. I zank you, *monsieur*."

Beatrice thought she heard a faint sigh of relief.

"And now, if you don't mind, I must get back to my browsing. You have some exquisite *objets* out zere, young man. But nozzing zat can rival zose marvelous *tartarughe*."

Beatrice's ears twitched. *Tartarughe?*

As their footsteps died away, she let out her pent-up

breath. Her body ached from being held in one position and her mind reeled. Had they been talking about the turtles all along? The turtles from the fountain? The Frenchman—Monsieur Cambriolage—worked for someone who was buying them? But he seemed like such a sweet old man. And the Italian, who was he?

Then her racing mind slammed on the brakes and a single word resounded in her head.

Fakes.

She took a moment to let the word sink in.

Monsieur Cambriolage had said something about fakes. What were his exact words? A rumor that the Italian was planning to sell him fakes . . .

The truth smacked Beatrice in the face. When the turtles had been wrenched off the fountain, perhaps the thief had immediately replaced them with replicas—excellent copies that no one had detected? Why hadn't she thought of it before?

But then, if that were the case, if the turtles had already been stolen, why would the Frenchman need to watch them be removed *again*? Questions bobbed around in her brain like apples in a barrel, but she had no time to sit pondering them. She had to get out of there.

She glanced at the precious book lying forgotten by her side. She could gaze at it all night, but she'd never understand a word. She needed help. She had to take it with her.

Beatrice didn't like the word *steal*. She refused to admit, even to herself, that she was stealing a historical document. *Borrow* was a much better word. She'd bring it back, eventually, so borrow was, truly, the more accurate term.

The more pressing issue was how to get it out unseen. Her handbag was barely big enough for a hanky; the book wouldn't fit inside in a million years. She'd have to smuggle it out under her clothes. She loosened her wraparound skirt and tucked the book in at her waist. She silently congratulated herself for choosing a loose-fitting blouse; it covered the bulge the diary made at her tummy.

Half expecting Signor Beak Nose or his sidekick Beef Suit to be lying in wait for her, Beatrice tiptoed down the spiral staircase and out of the library. When she saw that all was clear, she cautiously ambled through the palazzo's never-ending galleries. She tightened her stomach muscles and prayed the diary wouldn't slip out of her skirt as she made her way down the grand staircase and across the courtyard.

Just as she was about to step into the sweet freedom of the piazza, a husky voice sounded behind her. *"Signorina!"* She froze. Turning around in slow motion, she widened her eyes, hoping she didn't look as guilty as she felt.

"La tua borsa!" the doorman demanded, his hand out.

Beatrice stared back, uncomprehending.

"Your bag!" he barked.

Making as few movements as possible, she handed over her tiny purse and tried not to imagine the consequences for swiping a piece of the collection. Beads of sweat pricked at her forehead, and she held her breath, both out of nervousness and to keep the diary in place.

The guard yanked her bag open, revealing nothing more than a set of house keys and a folded ten-euro note. He roughly handed it back and waved her on.

She was about to let out an enormous sigh of relief but realized just in time that if she did, the diary would fall straight to the ground. Instead she took tiny sips of air and fought the urge to bolt straight for her building.

As she placed one faltering foot in front of the other, the smooth leather book began to slip lower and lower. She pressed her belly out as far as she could until she reached her door at last. She fished her keys out of her handbag with trembling fingers and fumbled with the lock, stepping inside just as the diary flopped onto the stone floor.

Late that night, perched in the loft above her bed, Beatrice sat at her desk with the diary open and her dad's massive dictionary at the ready.

She turned her attention to the diary with anticipation strumming at her heartstrings. But after half an hour, her excitement had turned to frustration and defeat. The old-fashioned handwriting, the faded ink, the complexity of the language: it was all too much for her, even with the help of a dictionary. She'd never be able to translate it, at least not on her own.

An image of her raven-haired Italian teacher floated before her eyes. If anyone could translate it, Ginevra could. But could she be trusted?

No. It was too risky.

Beatrice yawned, exhaustion hitting her like a tidal wave. It was hard to believe only last night she'd witnessed the theft of the turtles. It felt like a lifetime had passed since then.

She stumbled down the spiral staircase and slipped into bed, propping open the diary on her pillow. Struggling to keep her eyes open, she tried in vain to absorb the indecipherable words that had been scrawled all those centuries ago. Maybe if she stared at them long enough, their meaning would come to her in her dreams.

She turned a few more pages as the breeze from her window made the curtains dance. At last her eyelids could support their weight no longer. The diary slid off her pillow and landed open on the floor with a gentle *thunk*, rousing her momentarily. She reached down to grab it but it was just out of reach. The last thing she heard before yielding to sleep was the sound of brittle pages rustling under her bed.

fourteen

A HALF-AND-HALF PARTNER

"Mio fratello," lilted Ginevra's voice.

"Mio fratello," repeated Beatrice, trying to match her accent. *My brother.*

"Mia sorella."

"Mia sorella." My sister.

"Mio padr—" Ginevra's voice cracked on the Italian word for *father.*

Beatrice looked up. Ginevra, usually poised and composed, sat silently, her eyes cast down. Tears brimmed on her lower lids and one spilled over, plopping onto the page.

"Ginevra? What's wrong?"

"*Niente, niente,*"[1] she said, a wobble in her voice.

"It's okay," Beatrice assured her. "You can tell me."

For a long moment, Ginevra said nothing. Then her stoic facade crumbled. "It ees my father. . . ." She gulped, breaking her no-English rule for the first time. "He died a few months ago. I still . . . I still miss heem." She turned her face away.

Beatrice placed her hand on Ginevra's. "I'm so sorry." After a moment of silence, she added shyly, "I . . . I know what it's like. I lost my mom too."

Ginevra turned to Beatrice but didn't meet her gaze. "I don't know what's come over me. I have not cried een weeks." She ran two fingertips along her lower eyelids and took a deep breath. "*Continuiamo!*"[2] she sang, as if nothing had happened. "*Mio padre.*"

"*Mio padre,*" Beatrice repeated. She peeked at Ginevra out of the corner of her eye, but her teacher chirped on, the moment of weakness forgotten.

But for a second, it seemed an invisible wall between them had dissolved. Ginevra had—even if briefly—let her into her private world. Did she have

. . . .

1. "Nothing, nothing."
2. "Moving on!"

the courage to do the same? Again she had the urge to ask Ginevra for help translating the diary. It would be such a convenient solution to her dilemma.

But once more, something held her back, a faint *tap-tap-tap* on the inside of her skull. So she waited until, lesson over, she had kissed Ginevra good-bye on each cheek and watched her disappear down the stairs. Only then did she retrieve the diary from her bedroom floor, place it in a plastic bag, and slip it into her backpack. She needed help, and had a tiny idea where to find it.

Beatrice set off down the narrow streets in search of her new friend Marco. Okay, so he wasn't exactly her *friend*, but he'd helped her with the legend so maybe he'd give her a hand with the diary too.

She wandered the neighborhood, but there was no sign of him, or anyone. With a sinking feeling, she realized it was post-lunch naptime, that ghostly hour when the shops close and everyone goes home for a snooze, especially in the heat of midsummer.

She walked down Via del Portico d'Ottavia, past Signor Morello's shop, which was predictably closed. The streets were deserted but for the unavoidable tourists and a few stray cats—no olive-skinned, curly-haired boys in sight. Marco and his family were probably tucking into a heaping plate of homemade pasta about now, she thought with a twang of envy, remembering the meager peanut butter and jelly sandwich she'd gobbled down on her own.

"Hey, Beatrice!" called a familiar voice. She spun around to find the object of her thoughts locking a bike to a pole a block away. "I thought it was you," Marco said casually as he sauntered over. He sounded so American it was hard to believe he hadn't spent all his days in California, but his confident strut proved he was Roman, born and bred.

"Were you looking for me?" he asked, a flicker of amusement in his eyes.

Beatrice's color rose as she realized she was loitering right in front of his father's shop. He probably thought she had a crush on him and was waiting on his doorstep like a lovesick puppy. Her cheeks burned at the thought.

She decided to get right to the point. "As a matter of fact, I *was* looking for you," she said in her most businesslike voice. "I wanted to ask you a favor. I'm trying to translate something, but I'm not having much luck. I was wondering if you could, maybe, give me a hand?" By the time she got to the end of her speech, her confidence had melted. What made her think he'd be willing to help *her*? It was summer vacation; the last thing he'd want to do was translate something for a complete stranger.

"Sure, why not?" he answered, and her heart skipped a beat. "Why don't we grab a coffee and I can take a look at it."

"Perfect!"

Once they were seated in a deliciously air-conditioned café, Marco with an iced coffee and Beatrice with a blackberry juice, she pulled out the diary. She immediately kicked herself for not making photocopies and leaving the original at home. How would she explain what it was, and why she had it? She prayed he wouldn't ask.

"Wow, what's this?" he asked immediately, picking up the diary and leafing through it with a delicate touch.

She groaned silently. "Well . . . it's an antique diary I found . . . in a library." It was a simplified story, but a true one. "I'm translating it because . . ." She racked her brain but drew a blank.

"Because . . . ?"

". . . because I think it contains a clue to a mystery I'm trying to solve." The words tumbled out before she could stop them. Spoken aloud for the first time, they sounded a bit melodramatic.

"What kind of mystery?" Beneath a veneer of disbelief, Marco's eyes simmered with curiosity.

"I can't tell you that. At least, not yet."

He arched one eyebrow. "Let me get this straight: you want me to translate this antique book of yours, but you won't tell me why? Why should I help you at all?" he asked with a cheeky grin.

She couldn't tell if he was joking or serious. Maybe a little of both. He seemed willing to help, but not unless she told him the whole story. She didn't have much of a choice: it was him or no one.

"You promise you won't tell anyone?"

He looked serious, in spite of himself. "I promise."

"The Turtle Fountain has been attacked," she blurted out.

"What?" Marco nearly spat out his coffee.

"Bernini's turtles have been stolen off it."

"But I just rode past it ten minutes ago! It looked fine to me."

"They've been replaced with fakes—very convincing fakes."

"And you know this *how*?"

"I witnessed the theft myself."

Marco's jaw dropped as the words spilled out of Beatrice's mouth. She told him *everything*: how she'd seen a man in black wrench the turtles off the fountain Monday night, how she'd made the connection with the legend, how she'd snuck into the Mattei Palace where she stumbled across the diary and overheard the suspicious conversation in the library. She'd been reluctant to share her secrets, but now that they were out, she realized how much she'd been dying to share her discovery.

Marco furrowed his brow. Beatrice could practically read the doubt in his eyes as he considered the likelihood of her outlandish tale. She couldn't blame him for being skeptical. Even *she* hadn't believed it at first, and she'd seen it with her own eyes.

Sensing he'd never take her word for it, she dragged him out of the café and back to Piazza Mattei. It wasn't until, standing beside the fountain, they compared the position of the turtles to the photo in her guidebook that he reluctantly admitted she could be right.

"I've lived in this neighborhood my whole life," Marco said. "I've probably seen that fountain five thousand times, but I would never have noticed if you hadn't pointed it out."

"Well, the fakes are identical; it's just their positioning that gives them away. No one else seems to have noticed."

"Eventually they will. The next time the fountain is cleaned, if not sooner."

"But by then, whoever did this will be long gone—and the turtles with them. That's why I've got to solve this now, before it's too late!"

"Even if it's true—and I'm not saying it isn't," he added when she shot him a scowl, "what makes you think there's a clue in the diary? Or that what happened to the turtles has anything to do with that legend?"

"I can't explain it, but I keep getting these hunches, like the night the turtles were stolen and I had an urge to look out my window. And in the Mattei library, something made me search the upper level. It's like the diary was calling to me, leading me up there somehow."

Marco looked at her like she was a silly little girl

and a cold breeze hit her right in the heart. "Come on, what kind of clue could *plausibly* be in there? I mean, this diary was written four hundred years ago; the turtles were stolen two *days* ago."

Beatrice steeled herself, remembering the importance of her mission. "Look, I don't need you to believe me. I just need you to help me."

fifteen

DELVING INTO THE DIARY

Back in the café, in front of his second coffee, Marco turned the pages of the diary as if he were an archaeologist handling a long-lost sacred text. Meanwhile Beatrice twiddled her thumbs, wishing there were some way she could participate besides peeking over his shoulder at the indecipherable words. After what felt like ages, curiosity got the better of her.

"Well? Are there any clues?"

Marco scratched his mop of chestnut curls. He puffed his cheeks out and slowly released the air through pursed lips. "There could be, but I haven't found them yet."

"Well, what does it say?"

"It's pretty sad, actually. She writes about how miserable she is. It seems like the legend is true. She did not want to marry that duke."

"I knew it! Does she write about walling up the window?"

"No, not yet anyway. The beginning was a little boring, so I skipped ahead a bit. She keeps mentioning something about a secret room."

"A secret room?" Beatrice squealed. "What does she say about it?"

"Nothing specific. Just that she goes there to write in her diary, and get away from the husband she can't stand."

Beatrice went cold. She tried to imagine being married to a man she hated, having to hide from him. No wonder the duchess looked so miserable in her portrait. She was grateful she'd been born in a time when women were allowed to choose their own husbands. As romantic as life seemed back then, it couldn't have been easy being a woman.

"A secret room," she whispered, coming back to the present. "Did she say where it was? Was it in the palace?"

"She doesn't say, but she brings it up a lot." He gently thumbed through the diary. "I'm not sure you're going to find any clues in here, but it's pretty interesting. I've still got a ways to go."

Beatrice glanced at her watch; it was later than she thought.

"What time is it?" Marco asked. "Geez, I gotta go! I'm supposed to help my dad at the shop."

"Oh." Beatrice's enthusiasm deflated. "Look, don't worry about the rest, I'll find someone else."

"Listen," Marco said casually, "why don't I take the diary home with me tonight? I can write out the translation so you can read it yourself."

"What?" He had to be joking.

"That way I can get it done faster. I'll translate anything that seems important, word for word. If I find any clues, we can look into them tomorrow."

"*We?*"

"It seems to me you could use all the help you can get," he said with an impish grin.

She looked up at him from under a pair of furrowed brows.

"What are you afraid of? That I'm going to run off with the diary . . . or turn you in for pinching it?" he said with a wink.

She was embarrassed to admit it, but she *was*

worried. She'd only met Marco a few days ago. What did she really know about him? The diary was over four centuries old, and it wasn't hers. More important, it might hold a vital clue.

"Why are you so interested in helping me?" she asked, more suspicious than she'd like to admit.

"Are you kidding?" His voice was harsh with sarcasm. "I grew up in this neighborhood. My family has lived here for generations . . . for centuries! You moved here a month ago, and you're already in love with that fountain. Imagine how I feel about it! How could I *not* want to help?"

Beatrice felt ashamed. All the secrecy and snooping around were getting to her. "I'm sorry, I didn't mean . . . Of *course* you care about the fountain." She didn't want to let the diary out of her sight, but without someone to translate it, it was no use to her at all. It didn't take long to take stock of her options. "Okay, you can borrow it, but just for one night. You think you can translate the rest by tomorrow?"

"Sure," he said. "It's not that long. I'll just translate the important bits."

"Cool. Hey, listen," she said shyly, "you won't tell anybody about it, will you?"

"Course not. It'll be our secret. I promise!" he added when she didn't look convinced.

She smiled inwardly. She was surprised at how good it felt to have someone else in on her secret. "Okay," she said in a shaky voice. "Tomorrow morning I have my Italian lesson. Wanna meet right after lunch, here at this café?"

"Sure. Two o'clock?"

"Perfect." She wrapped the diary back in the plastic bag and reluctantly handed it over. "Be careful with it. It's over four hundred years old."

"I'll guard it with my life." His voice was hushed with solemnity, but he had the look of a rascal in his eyes. The corners of her lips twitched as she tried to suppress a smile. "Anyway," he said, "I'm used to handling old stuff from working at my dad's shop."

"Of course." Beatrice recalled the treasure trove of ancient and mysterious objects.

"Well, I'd better run; we got a huge lot of Roman coins in this morning and I have to put them in order before the shop closes. *A domani!*"[1] he called as he ran off.

. . . .

1. "See you tomorrow!"

"*A domani!*" she echoed, hoping she hadn't just made the biggest mistake of her life.

As Beatrice walked home, she felt like there was an octopus juggling inside her belly. She was itching to continue her investigations, but without the diary she didn't know where to go next. As if of their own accord, her feet led her straight to her father's study, where she pulled several books onto the floor. She had to laugh: whenever she needed answers, she automatically reached for books. She was her father's daughter.

Half an hour later, as she leafed through a massive illustrated volume called *The Renaissance Palaces of Rome*, full of complicated floor plans and diagrams, she sat up with a start. The facade of the Mattei Palace stared at her from the page. She found the accompanying text and gobbled it up.

In order to strengthen their dominance in the city, the Mattei family built a stronghold of four connected palaces in rione Sant'Angelo, just outside the Jewish Ghetto. The first palace, Palazzo Giacomo

Mattei, was built in 1525 utilizing the ruins of the first-century BC Theater of Balbus as a foundation. Over the following century, other branches of the Mattei family built palaces in the same block, each one attached to the other. The result was the formidable Isola Mattei, a self-contained "island" of Mattei power taking up an entire city block. A number of the structure's walls were built directly on top of the curving arrangement of foundation stones of the ancient theater below. This can be seen clearly in the floor plan of Palazzo Giacomo Mattei, in the southwest corner of the Isola.

The largest and grandest palace in the Isola is Palazzo Mattei di Giove, built at the height of Mattei glory in the early 1600s. Asdrubale Mattei decorated the palace's courtyard with works of ancient and Renaissance art, many of which remain today. Of the four palaces that make up Isola Mattei, only Palazzo Giacomo Mattei *remains in private hands; it is inhabited by members of the Mattei family to this day.*

As Beatrice scrutinized the floor plan, a tremor of excitement shot through her, but all she saw was a jumble of rooms and corridors. Glancing back at the text, one line in particular caught her attention: *A number of the structure's walls were built directly on top of the curving arrangement of foundation stones of the ancient theater below.*

She focused on the lower left corner of the floor plan, the area that showed Palazzo Giacomo Mattei. It was an incomprehensible maze of lines going in different directions. Still, as she scrutinized it, trying to take in just the shapes, a pattern emerged. Here and there she could pick out short little walls that formed a sweeping convex curve.

She was still crouched over the enormous volume, her face inches from the page, when her father came home. "Nose in a book as usual!" he exclaimed, making Beatrice jump.

"Dad!" she sang, her voice giddy with triumph. She sprang up and flung herself into his arms.

"What is it?" he asked, returning her bear hug. "You look like you've just discovered the Rosetta Stone!"

"Even better!" she whooped. She was bursting with excitement over the adventure she found herself in, and pride at how she was puzzling her way through it. She simply couldn't bear to hide it from her father for one more second.

He glanced down at the open tome at her feet. "A discovery in a history book? Now there's a girl after my own heart."

Beatrice leaped at the encouragement. "Well, remember the other night when—"

A shrill ring sounded from her father's pocket.

"Just a minute, sweet pea," he said, checking the screen. "This is the academy; I've got to take it. Be a darling and go put the water on for the pasta."

"But, Dad, this is important."

"So is this. I won't be a minute." He ushered her out of his study. "Professor Archer speaking," he said, and closed the door.

The excitement drained out of her like milk from a ball of fresh mozzarella. She shuffled toward the kitchen, grabbing her guidebook from the hall table. After placing a pot of water on the cooktop and lighting the gas with a *clack-clack-whoosh*, she flopped down at the kitchen table. Flipping through her guidebook, she easily located the page for the Theater of Balbus, but there was barely any information. Just a few paragraphs and one measly diagram.

She traced her finger idly along the left side of the diagram, marked as the cavea, the curving section where the spectators sat. Something about it was vaguely familiar. She skimmed the text for enlightening clues but there was nothing new. Then she saw the last line: *This site is not accessible to the public.* She closed the guidebook with a sigh. So much for her big discovery.

Her dad straggled in, looking as dejected as she felt.

"What's wrong?"

"There's been a security breach at the academy," he said, rubbing his forehead, "in the history department's ancient artifacts collection. Nothing seems to be missing, but it's still worrying. As head of the department, I'm responsible, of course."

"But you just started last week. They can't blame *you*!"

"They can and they will. If anything serious were

to happen, it could cost me my job."

Beatrice's blood ran cold. After all her complaining about moving to Rome, she'd never felt so alive as in these last few days. The thought of packing up and heading back to Boston, mystery unsolved, would be like admitting defeat before she'd even begun.

"But don't you go worrying your little red head about it!" he said with forced cheerfulness. "Let's get dinner on the table."

As they sat over their rigatoni, Beatrice flicked listlessly through her guidebook and her dad leafed through the evening paper.

"So, what was it you wanted to tell me?" he asked, not taking his eyes off the paper.

Beatrice was tempted to shrug it off. He had his own worries and there was always the possibility that her latest discovery would lead nowhere. But then again, if he couldn't help her solve this puzzle, no one could.

"W-well," she stammered, "did you know that underneath the buildings on the other side of the piazza are the ruins of an ancient Roman theater?"

"I seem to recall reading something of that nature," he said distractedly.

"The Theater of Balbus, first century BC!" she proclaimed.

"Interesting," he muttered, still engrossed in his reading.

"Well, I was thinking that maybe—"

"My god!" her father exclaimed.

"What is it?"

"There was a break-in at Palazzo Rospigliosi. A painting by Botticelli was stolen!"

Suddenly Beatrice's appetite was gone. "When? How?"

He scanned the article, translating the gist of it. "Late last night, it seems. The family is at their seaside home for the summer. Only the housekeeper was there, and she apparently slept through the whole thing. Discovered it was missing this morning."

Two works of art disappear on two consecutive nights, plus a security breach at the academy: it couldn't be a coincidence.

"What a shame. Such an exquisite work, even though, if it were up to me, it would be on display in a public museum, not shut up in a private collection. Still, a terrible loss for the Rospigliosi family. It's been in their collection for centuries."

Beatrice finally found her tongue. "You don't think it could be connected to—" She stopped short, waiting for the inevitable interruption.

"Connected to what?"

"To . . . what happened to the fountain the other night?"

"I don't follow you."

"The Turtle Fountain . . . ?" she clarified.

"Oh, that! You're not still hung up about that nightmare, are you? Silly goose!" He tousled her hair and began clearing the table.

Beatrice bristled. When the turtles were revealed to be fakes and Bernini's originals long gone, maybe then he'd start taking her seriously.

She just hoped it wouldn't have to come to that.

sixteen
A PASSAGEWAY AND
A HIDING PLACE

Beatrice sat in the café, sipping an iced tea and tapping her foot nervously. She swiveled around every time someone walked through the door, but two o'clock came and went with no sign of Marco. He's just running late, she assured herself. Italian family lunches were elaborate and long. To pass the time, she scrawled in her notebook what she'd learned so far:

The turtles were stolen off the fountain late Monday
night (July 26) by a tall, thin man, possibly with a
shaved head and arm tattoos.

The turtles were *apparently* replaced with high-quality fakes.

A certain Monsieur Cambriolage is buying the turtles on behalf of an unidentified "client." This client is afraid of forgeries.

So many unknowns. So much of what she was going on was intuition and guesswork. She jotted down a few questions:

Who was the Italian man in the library?

Who is Cambriolage working for?

Where are the turtles now?

She underlined the last question. If she could discover that, nothing else mattered.

A glance at her watch showed twenty after two. Where was Marco? Maybe he'd forgotten about the appointment? No, not possible.

At half past, her worry turned to dread. Her mind conjured the worst possible scenario: Marco had stolen the diary, and he wasn't coming back. How could she have been so naive to trust a virtual stranger? She'd been taken in by his easy smile and warm eyes but he was nothing but a liar and a thief. Just as tears of frustration sprang to her eyes, the door creaked open and Marco strutted in with a rakish grin, the diary under his arm.

Beatrice's heart flooded with relief. She hopped off her chair and nearly threw her arms around him, catching herself just in time. Instead she gave him the customary two-cheek kiss.

"Sorry I'm late! My mom made me wash all the dishes. Sometimes I wish I had an Italian mom—they never make their sons do housework!"

Beatrice felt a stab of envy. Italian or American, any mom was better than none.

"No worries," she said, with more composure than she felt. "So? Did you manage to finish it?"

"Yep. I was up till three, but I read the whole thing."

"And did you translate it?"

"Well, not every *single* entry, but all the interesting ones, and there were loads of interesting ones." He took out a spiral notebook along with the diary and handed them over triumphantly. "You can read it for yourself while I get a *caffè*."

Beatrice seized the notebook and practically tore off the cover. More than half the pages were filled with small, neat writing. Her eyes flitted here and there, reading snippets of entries. She wished she could read them all at once, but she forced herself to slow down and start from the beginning. With a trembling hand, she turned to the first page and read:

8 February 1594

As I prepare for bed, I cannot help but go over the events of the day, and it makes me weep to think about the cruelty of the duke—the brute that destiny has forced me to call Husband. If only my father could have saved me from this wretched fate. We've been married nearly six years, and I have yet to produce an heir. For this, he has come to despise me.

So here I am, the most miserable lady in Rome, with a husband who makes my life a nightmare. Yesterday, he caught me

*writing in this diary and threw it across
the room. He has taken all my friends
and family from me, refuses to let me
leave the palace or see anyone. My only
companion is this small book in which to
confide my thoughts. And now he wants to
deny me that as well! But I will defy him;
I will find a way to write in secret. I
must or I fear I will lose my mind.*

The entries were sporadic, often with several months between them. The first dozen or so were similar, filled with Caterina's complaints about her marriage and life. By the time Beatrice had read about a quarter of Marco's translation, she was close to tears. The duchess had had such a miserable existence, and in a way it was all because of that fountain. It didn't seem right that something so lovely should have caused— even indirectly—so much pain.

But as moved as Beatrice was by Caterina's words, she had a rising sense of dread that there would be nothing helpful in the diary after all. She pressed on, and after a few more uneventful entries, she read:

27 November 1598

Today I made an odd discovery. I was in the palace library, searching for a book to read. In this miserable existence that is my life, reading is my only solace. That, and expressing my thoughts in this diary.

Muzio is in the countryside touring his estates; otherwise I would never have had the chance to find what I did. I was searching in a part of the library I had never explored before, because the shelves are difficult to reach, behind the globe in the corner, with very poor light. I had to light a candle to be able to see the titles of the books, even though it was full day.

My eye spotted a slender volume of Aristotle, and I had to reach awkwardly behind the globe to grasp it. But the books were packed so tightly that it wouldn't budge. Beside the Aristotle was a large, plain book, with no title on the spine. I doubt I would have touched it had it not been beside the one I wanted.

I tugged the book, hoping to dislodge the Aristotle, when I heard a loud noise. A moment later, as if a hinge had been sprung, an entire section of the bookcase shifted. It was a concealed door, and scarcely knowing what I was doing, I pulled it toward me. It must have been long unused for it took a good deal of effort to pull it back far enough to look inside.

I peered into the small opening, but all I could see was a steep stone staircase descending into blackness. I dared not venture further for fear of what might have been lurking down in the darkness. I replaced the bookcase as it was and have spoken of it to no one. Yet I cannot get that hidden doorway out of my mind. Where could it possibly lead?

"I was in that library! I was there!" Beatrice marveled. "I can't believe there was a hidden doorway so near me. Do you think it has anything to do with that secret room you were talking about?"

Marco's eyes twinkled. "Keep reading."

5 March 1599

If Muzio's cruelty were directed only toward myself, perhaps I could forgive him, but he is heartless to all. When he flies into a rage, woe to anyone in his path. All the servants are terrified of him and he has them whipped for the slightest offense.

I try to be kind to the servants, but decorum dictates I show them neither friendship nor even gratitude for their work. Cut off as I am from social interaction, I value them more than simply as laborers. The housekeeper, Assunta, is one of the oldest servants in the household, and has been employed here for more than half a century. In fact, she came here when old Duke Giacomo Mattei, Muzio's grandfather, first built the palace.

Assunta is an odd character, tough

on the outside, setting a strict example for the other servants, but with a soft heart underneath. I found her crying a few weeks ago. She was so worried I would be angry with her for showing emotion while working. If Muzio had seen her, he would have been furious.

I asked her why she was crying. She refused to speak at first, but at last she revealed that her youngest grandson had died fighting for the papal army in the north. I comforted her as best I could, and since then we have become friends, at least as much as servant and mistress can be. I shudder to think what Muzio would do to me—or to her—if he found out.

16 April 1599

Yesterday, while I was embroidering, I invited Assunta to my rooms to keep me company. We sat talking for hours, and in the course of conversation, she revealed something most intriguing.

When the old duke first built the

palace over fifty years ago, he had a secret chamber constructed underground with a hidden passageway connecting it to one of the rooms. It was richly decorated and fitted with every luxury, or so she had heard. The duke would go there when he wanted utter privacy. Assunta had never seen it herself, as it was a jealously guarded secret. The only servant who had ever seen it was the duke's valet, who cleaned the room himself. No one else knew of its existence, not even the old duchess.

At that time, the duke's valet was Assunta's sweetheart, and later her husband. It was he who told her about the hidden chamber, swearing her to secrecy. She never knew exactly where it was, only that it was somewhere underneath the palace.

On his deathbed, Duke Giacomo passed the secret on to his son, Muzio's father. The secret was meant to pass this way, from father to son, duke to duke, but Muzio's father died in a hunting accident

when Muzio was still a child, so he never
had a chance to reveal the location to
him. Not long after, Assunta's husband
died as well, and the location of the
secret room was lost. Assunta is the only
person alive who knows of its existence, a
secret she has kept for over thirty years.

I cannot imagine why she chose to
tell me, except perhaps because I am the
only member of the family to show her any
kindness. I pretended her story was of
no interest to me, but in truth, I was
fascinated by every word.

I believe—no, I am convinced—that the
hidden door I discovered by accident leads
to that secret room. I'm tempted to seek
it out myself, to have a place to escape
Muzio's rages, where I can write or read in
peace. Still, I am terrified at the thought
of what restless spirits I might encounter
if I had the courage to descend the dark
staircase into that long-unvisited chamber.
And worse, what would happen if I got lost
and couldn't find my way out?

Beatrice shuddered. She visualized Caterina sinking into the dark unknown, imagining ghosts around every corner. She read on.

25 April 1599

    I have decided to search for the secret room. I'm terrified but also exhilarated. It's the first time since my marriage that I am truly excited about something, and if only for this reason, I am determined to find it. I considered asking Assunta to assist me, but thought better of it. If I involve her and we are found out, she could be dismissed, or worse.

    No, I will do it alone. Naturally I will take a candle, but that will not be enough if I lose my way, so I've decided to take a large spool of embroidery thread. I will tie one end to the bookcase and unravel it as I go. When I need to find my way out, I will just follow the thread.

Beatrice was giddy with anticipation. She turned the page, certain it would reveal directions to the secret room. But as she read the next entry, and then the next, there was no further mention of it. Caterina just kept on writing, as if nothing had changed.

Beatrice looked at Marco with disappointment. "Did she find the room or not?"

"Oh, she found it all right. See?" He flipped ahead several pages and indicated a few other entries. "She mentions it here, and here. But read this first." He flipped ahead farther still.

5 December 1600

I am afraid that Muzio is beginning to suspect. I spend nearly all of my time in the library these days, searching for new books and sneaking down to the secret room to read or write. More than once, he has asked me where I've been, and I have had to lie.

I worry about his wrath if he were to discover what I am doing, so I try to go there only when he is not at home, or early in the morning, when I know he is asleep. I cannot bear the thought of giving it up altogether. Since I came here, I finally have a place I feel is truly my own, where I can get away and be alone with my own thoughts. Not to mention, this underground room is the perfect hiding place for my diary—he'll never find it here.

"'He'll never find it here,'" Beatrice repeated. "'He'll never find it *here*'!" Time seemed to stop, and Beatrice sat immobile, staring into space. A warm sensation seeped through her pores as her thoughts shifted into place like the pieces of a jigsaw puzzle. She didn't even realize Marco was talking.

"Beatrice? Hey, Beatrice! What planet are you on?"

She jolted back to the present to find Marco shaking her shoulder. She turned to him with triumph in her darkening eyes. "I know where they're hidden," she announced.

"Where what are hidden?"

"The turtles." She spoke with a still, quiet voice and Marco gaped at her with a look of bewilderment. But she just sat there, smiling to herself.

"Where?" he finally burst out.

"In Caterina's secret room, of course."

seventeen

CATERINA'S CURSE

Beatrice felt strangely serene. She would have expected to be jumping up and down, clapping her hands. Instead she sat calmly as the picture in her mind came into focus.

She'd been led to that diary by some mysterious force, just as she'd been led to Caterina's portrait. And now it all made sense. What better hiding place for the turtles than a secret room?

"Yeah, that *could* be," Marco ventured, "but it doesn't seem very likely. I mean, even if that room still exists—which is doubtful after four hundred years—how would the thieves know about it?"

"Maybe it's described in some historical document?"

Marco rolled his eyes. "Not likely."

His words were like a bucket of cold water dumped on her head. A moment ago she'd been convinced, but two words from him had her doubting her instincts again. Was he right—was she jumping to conclusions?

Still, her heart was tugging her rational mind back around. "No, I'm sure of it," she said. "This is the clue I've been looking for."

"If you say so," said Marco with a curling lip.

Beatrice's stomach tightened. It was cool having someone to throw ideas around with, but when she did things on her own, at least no one scoffed at her ideas. It was bad enough that her father believed she was delusional, she thought, recalling their conversation from the night before.

"Oh, that reminds me!" she exclaimed. "A famous painting—a Botticelli—was stolen last night!"

"Really? From where?"

"Some rich family's private collection—Rospi-something or other. You don't think it could have anything to do with the disappearance of the turtles, do you?"

Marco considered for a moment before shaking his head. "Naaah, there's always break-ins in summer. So many people go out of town, burglars figure it's not as risky. And usually they get away with it. Practically everyone I know has had their place robbed at least once."

"But this wasn't just some random burglary. They took one *specific* work of art. Whoever took it must have known it was there."

He shrugged. "Maybe they did. Still doesn't mean it has anything to do with the turtles."

But it did. Because they were both priceless, centuries-old works of art. It couldn't just be a coincidence.

"I'm starting to think we should go to the police."

Marco chuckled. "Honestly, Beatrice, don't bother—unless you like to waste your time." Before she had a chance to protest, he continued. "First of all, they won't take you seriously. They wouldn't take *me* seriously, and I'm from here. And secondly, they've got enough to do, fighting the mafia and dealing with violent crime. By the time they got around to looking into our case, we'd be out of college already."

Beatrice sighed. He was probably right. It's not like

they were in a small town where the worst thing the police had to deal with was some old lady's missing Pekingese.

Her mind flicked, almost instinctively, to her father. Could she try mentioning it to him again? Would he listen to her now that she had a theory? She pictured him smiling disdainfully and laughing off her childish ideas, and stuffed down the thought. Looked like she had no choice. Whether she liked it or not, she and Marco were in this alone.

"So," Marco said, "can you believe that part about how Caterina cursed the Mattei family?"

"What?"

"Here." He flipped toward the back of the notebook. "Read this."

15 October 1601

This will be my last entry.

I have no other choice. Muzio has won. He has discovered my secret at last. I cannot pretend to be surprised; I knew it was only a matter of time. When you live in a house with dozens of servants, you can seldom keep a secret for long.

Three days ago, after a long morning
of writing, I was emerging from the
underground chamber through the library
passageway. I had my candle as usual,
although by now I know my way so well, I
could walk it blindfolded. As I ascended,
I noticed a light coming from the top
of the staircase. I am always careful
to close the door to the library behind
me, so I knew there could be no other
explanation: someone had found me out and
was waiting for me.

For a moment I considered turning
around and running back down the stairs,
but I soon grasped the futility and even
danger in that idea: there's no other way
out that I know of, so I would have had
to venture out at some point. And what
if whoever was waiting for me (although
I had little doubt who) would lock me in
forever?

It was therefore more terror than
bravery that led me to continue my ascent,
although I had the quickness of mind to

hide the diary before I reached the top. I
slipped it under my voluminous skirts

Beatrice took a sharp intake of breath, remembering how she too had hid the very same diary under her (albeit less voluminous) skirt when she had snuck it out of the palace.

and when I reached the doorway, just as
I had suspected, Muzio was waiting for
me. I cannot bear to relive what happened
next. I will write only that his rage at
discovering my deceit, even for something
so innocent, was beyond my imaginings.
Tomorrow I will hide this diary in the
darkest corner of the library where he
will never find it, and where, perhaps
many years from now, someone will discover
it and read it and pity me.

I know he will never again allow me
a moment's solitude or freedom, even to
scrawl down my thoughts in this simple
book. I am taking a risk by writing this

now, locked in my dressing room in the
middle of the night.

He thinks he can control me, and
perhaps he can, but he cannot control
my thoughts. And tonight I have only one
thought, one wish, one desire: to curse
him. I will go to my grave cursing the
name of Mattei. I call upon whatever is
just and vengeful in the heavens to bring
down destruction on every branch of this
evil family and on their descendants in
perpetuity, until they are extinguished.

"Whoa, that's intense." Beatrice took a moment to let it sink in. "Well, the Frenchman said they'd been cursed. Maybe that's why the Mattei family is dying out, why they're selling everything they own. It's kind of ironic, actually."

"It's more than irony; it's poetic justice," Marco spat out. "You know, it was the Mattei who controlled the gates of the Ghetto."

"What?" Beatrice thought she knew everything about the Mattei family. Her father was right; there was no such thing as too much research.

"C'mon, I'll show you."

They grabbed their things and walked the short blocks to Piazza Mattei. As they skirted down Via della Reginella, Marco pointed out something Beatrice hadn't noticed before: a tiny mosaic of the Star of David embedded into the wall of a building. Beside it was a rough bas-relief menorah. "This means we're near one of the Ghetto's original entrances."

The street opened onto Piazza Mattei. On the left stood Beatrice's building; straight ahead was Palazzo Giacomo Mattei. Marco pointed to the ground. "See that?"

On one corner of the narrow street sat a marble slab. "This is the base of the gate that used to be here." He kicked it for emphasis. "During the confinement of the Jews, the pope gave the Mattei family control of this gate. They charged the Jews a toll to come in or out. The Jews got poorer and the Matteis got richer."

Beatrice's stomach turned. "How do you know all this stuff?"

"Well, we're Jewish. My dad's family has lived in the Ghetto for centuries, and as you know, he's obsessed with history. I grew up hearing these stories. Over four hundred years later," Marco said, scowling at the palace, "and the Mattei are finally getting what they deserve. They're losing everything."

They're losing everything. . . . His words echoed in her mind like a half-remembered dream. They were the same words the Frenchman had used when they were waiting in line together. Without realizing it, Marco had given her a missing piece of the puzzle.

eighteen

THE SUBTLE ART OF
EAVESDROPPING

"That's it!" Beatrice gasped, her eyes brimming with triumph. "They stole the turtles themselves!"

"Who did?"

"The Mattei family!"

"What? What are you talking about?"

"Don't you see? The Matteis are destitute . . . they're losing everything—you said it yourself. But the turtles, right outside their front door, are the work of Bernini; they're worth a fortune. They sell those turtles and they'll be rich again. They sell those turtles and they'll have enough money to keep their palace!"

"I guess that's *one* possibility," Marco allowed.

"It's more than a possibility! It makes perfect sense!" she insisted, her words struggling to keep up with her racing thoughts. "When I was in the Mattei library, I heard an Italian man—probably one of the Matteis—talking with the Frenchman I'd met earlier, Monsieur Cambriolage. He's working for whoever is buying the turtles, I'm sure of it."

Marco threw her a shrewd look. "What exactly did you overhear in that library?"

Beatrice closed her eyes, recalling the hushed conversation. "Well, the Italian man said he wanted to talk in private. He said something about not wanting them to be seen together and asked Cambriolage why he hadn't waited for their appointment."

"Did they say when this appointment was?"

"Not that I can remember."

"What else did they say?"

Beatrice closed her eyes again. "Cambriolage said he'd heard a rumor that the Italian was planning to sell him fakes. That's when I first realized the turtles had been replaced with replicas!"

"Wait a minute. I thought you saw them being switched yourself?"

"Well, not exactly," she admitted. "I saw the turtles being ripped off, then I went to wake up my dad, but by the time we got back to the window, they'd already been replaced and the thief was gone."

"So you didn't actually *see* them being replaced with fakes? Then how can you be so sure these aren't the real turtles?"

"You noticed a difference yourself!" Beatrice countered. "Anyway, the Italian man was very offended by the mention of the fakes. Too offended, like he was trying to hide something. He told Cambriolage that if he didn't trust him, he could witness the theft himself, and be there in person for the handoff." Beatrice paused. "That's the part that doesn't make sense, though." She furrowed her brow. "They were acting like the turtles hadn't been stolen yet, when I *saw* it happen Monday night."

Marco drew in his lips. "But maybe they weren't actually stolen? What if what you witnessed was a trial run? What if the thief had to make sure he'd be *able* to detach the turtles before they could go ahead with the plan? Then he put them back until he was ready to steal them for real. That would explain why the positioning is off. And it would mean the *real* theft hasn't happened yet."

"But if that were the case," argued Beatrice, "what did he put into the bags he strapped onto his scooter?"

"I dunno, it could have been anything! His tools, maybe?" He looked up at the fountain. "Look, they may be in a different position, but like you said, the Italian guy told the French guy he could witness the theft himself, so it *can't* have happened yet."

"Listen, I know what I saw. And I saw those turtles being *stolen*."

"All you saw was the thief take the turtles off the fountain. You can't possibly be sure he didn't put them right back on."

Marco's skepticism was a carnival mirror, magnifying her own self-doubt, and distorting her theories into ridiculous fantasy. She burned at his flippant dismissal of her ideas and opened her mouth to defend them.

Before she had the chance, a beat-up motor scooter buzzed past them into the square spewing a cloud of black smoke. Marco coughed resentfully, waving a hand in front of his face. "*Che schifo!*[1] There are laws

. . . .

1. "How disgusting!"

against driving a *motorino* with emissions like that. They pollute the environment!"

The grimy red scooter screeched to a halt in front of the Mattei Palace and a lanky youth slid off. With intricately inked arms, he reached up and removed his helmet to reveal a perfectly shaved head.

Beatrice's eyes widened. She grabbed Marco's hand to pull him behind the fountain. At the touch of his palm against hers, a zap of electricity ran up her arm. She dropped his hand as if it had burned her. "It's him, it's him, it's him!" she whispered, trying to ignore her tingling fingertips and focus instead on the scene unfolding before them.

"Who?" Marco asked, goggling between Beatrice and the object of her gaping eyes.

"The thief!" she nearly shrieked. "The turtle thief!" She crouched behind the fountain, beckoning to Marco to do the same.

"But how do you know? Didn't you say his face was covered with a ski mask when you saw him?"

"Shhh! Yes, but I saw the same guy prowling around the piazza the night I first arrived. Same shaved head, same tattoos: I *know* it's him. Anyway, I recognize his scooter."

"You're *sure* it's the same guy?"

"Positive."

Marco squatted down beside her, and the two of them watched the thief march up to the towering doors of the Mattei Palace, helmet tucked cockily under one arm. As the gangly young man jabbed the door buzzer, Beatrice and Marco shared a corner-of-the-eye glance.

"I told you the Matteis were mixed up in this!" she hissed.

"I never said they weren't."

The man pressed the buzzer again, leaning on it for a good five seconds. When he still didn't get a response, he whipped out his cell phone and punched a few keys.

"This is our chance!" whispered Marco excitedly. The mysterious arrival of their presumed thief seemed to have jolted him into action. Gone was Marco the doubter, and in his place was Marco the doer.

"What are you going to do?"

"I'm going to find out what he's up to." Marco's eyes darted around the square, then flicked back to the thin man. He was still standing, cell phone to ear, apparently waiting for someone to pick up.

Across the piazza, the door of Beatrice's building

swung open and out tottered old Signora Costaguti, leading her white fluff ball of a dog on a leash. Marco hopped up and trotted in her direction, Beatrice following close behind.

"Signora, come sta?"[2]

"Wait, *you* know Signora Costaguti?" Beatrice asked.

"Of course he does!" the old woman exclaimed with a smile. "I buy all my antiques from Signor Morello. Wouldn't trust anyone else."

"Signora, mi potrebbe prestare Artemisia?" Marco asked hurriedly, indicating the yapping dog. *"Solo qui in piazza, due secondi!"*[3]

"D'accordo,"[4] she said, nonplussed. "Wait! Better take this!" She handed him a plastic bag accompanied by a telltale raise of the eyebrow.

Marco smirked and stuffed the bag into his pocket. "You stay here," he said to Beatrice with a look of warning.

"What are you up to?" Beatrice demanded in a harsh whisper.

. . . .

2. "Signora, how are you?"

3. "Signora, can I borrow Artemisia? Just here in the piazza, two seconds!"

4. "All right."

"I know what I'm doing. Trust me!" he said through gritted teeth and scurried off.

Her eyes followed Marco across the square as he maneuvered the dog toward the thief, who was jabbering down the phone and gesticulating wildly. It was too far away to hear what he was saying, even if she could have understood.

". . . don't you think?"

"Hmm?" Beatrice said, turning back to Signora Costaguti. She blushed, realizing she'd missed whatever the old lady had asked her.

"It's a lovely day for a stroll, don't you think?" the old lady repeated sharply.

The truth was it was scorching. Anyone with any sense would stay inside with the air-conditioning on full blast on a day like this. But Beatrice merely nodded absently. She struggled to engage her elderly neighbor in conversation while simultaneously keeping tabs on Marco out of the corner of her eye. He made a comic sight, edging closer and closer to the thief while the dog pulled in the opposite direction, eager to explore all her favorite sniffing spots.

When Artemisia finally let Marco lead her toward the Mattei Palace, she abruptly hunkered down on her furry haunches, preparing to relieve herself then and there. Serves him right, thought Beatrice, suppressing a giggle. But to her surprise, Marco actually looked pleased with the turn of events. He pulled out the plastic bag with a satisfied grin and, once Artemisia had finished her business, he knelt to clean it up. As he carefully scooped up the dog poo, he kept one ear cocked toward the thief, who was still engrossed in his phone call.

"How are your lessons with Ginevra going?"

"Ginevra?" Suddenly the old lady had Beatrice's complete attention. "You know Ginevra *too*?" Beatrice was starting to think Signora Costaguti was personally acquainted with the entire city.

"Ah, well, when you've lived in one place as long as I have," she said with a smile, as if divining Beatrice's thought. "No, I don't know her personally. But when your father told me you needed a tutor, I made a few inquiries at the university where I used to teach, and I was given her name. She's had some recent family misfortunes, so I heard. I thought it charitable to help her find a job—keep her out of trouble."

"Trouble?" Beatrice raised an intrigued eyebrow. "What do you mean, trouble?"

But before she had a chance to learn more, Marco was standing in front of her with a wide grin on his dimpled face, Artemisia panting by his feet. *"Grazie, signora,"* he said, slightly out of breath.

"Grazie a te, Marco. I'm getting a bit old to bend down and clean up her little messes, so your gesture is much appreciated," she said, taking the dog's leash. "Now stay out of mischief, you two," she added with a look that said she knew very well they'd do no such thing, and stalked off.

Beatrice was still digesting what Signora Costaguti had said, but Marco was clearly bursting with news. "Did you hear anything? Anything important?" she asked.

"That guy, he's got an appointment with whoever was on the other end of that phone call. I missed most of the conversation, but I did hear one thing: he'll be at Via Giulia number 98, tomorrow at one-something in the afternoon."

"Where's Via Giulia?"

"About a ten-minute walk from here."

"I wonder what he's up to . . ."

"Well"—Marco shrugged—"there's only one way to find out."

"You mean like . . . stake him out?" A bubble of nervous excitement popped in her belly.

"We go down to Via Giulia at one o'clock tomorrow afternoon—if we have to wait around a bit, no big deal—we find building number 98, and we see what happens."

"What if somebody sees us?"

"So what? Who's going to notice a couple of kids?"

"But didn't he see you just now? You were cleaning up dog poo practically right under his nose," she said with a snort.

"He was way too occupied with his phone call to notice me. We've got to at least try. Whatever happened with the turtles, we both agree they're in danger. For all we know they could be on their way to France tomorrow!"

"You're right," said Beatrice grimly. "The Mattei family may be ruined, but we can't let them ruin our fountain."

nineteen

APPOINTMENT ON VIA GIULIA

The next morning Beatrice could barely sit still during her lesson. She was both thrilled and petrified at the prospect of lying in wait for a thief and his accomplices.

Ginevra, back to her cool and collected self, was teaching her to conjugate regular verbs. Ordinarily Beatrice would have jumped at the chance to learn something so advanced, but today she had other things on her mind. The unrelenting heat didn't help. It seemed to get hotter every day, if that were possible.

Once the lesson was finally over, she took a cool shower and had to skip lunch to make her appointment with Marco at a quarter to one. They set off for Via Giulia, crossing Via Arenula, the western boundary of the Ghetto. Beatrice felt a tingle of guilt for leaving the neighborhood against her father's orders, mixed with a zap of excitement that she was traipsing around Rome on the trail of an international art thief. Could this really be her life?

After a short walk, they reached Via Giulia. The street stretched out before them, long and straight, an unexpected thoroughfare in a city full of narrow, meandering alleys. They walked a ways in silence until Beatrice piped up, "Hey, I forgot to tell you something."

"What?"

"Well, I was doing a little research the other night, and I read that the Mattei Palace was built directly on top of the ruins of an ancient site, the Theater of Balbus."

"That's interesting, I guess. But what does it mean for us?"

"Don't you see? The ruins are right under the palace! I looked it up in my guidebook, but they're closed to the public. Caterina's secret room has got to be down there somewhere."

Marco's eyes widened. "Yes! It has to be!"

Beatrice did a double take. He agreed with her—it was a miracle.

"Now it makes sense why she wrote—" He stopped short.

"Why she wrote what?"

"Hang on," he said, "if the ruins are closed to the public, how are we supposed to get in?"

"Who knows? I had a hard enough time getting into the palace during the public auction viewing. What were you about to say?"

"Nothing important," he said dismissively. "Even if we did manage to get into the ruins," he continued, the cynical note creeping back into his voice, "I doubt we'd find anything."

Beatrice opened her mouth to disagree but Marco yammered on. "And even if the secret room is in the ruins like you say, that doesn't mean anything's hidden there. I bet no one's been down there in centuries."

A nasty mix of suspicion and outrage gurgled in Beatrice's belly. She was about to object to his line of reasoning when she noticed the building numbers were now in the 90s. They had to be close, so she decided not to press the point.

The palaces on Via Giulia were colossal, some stretching the entire length of the block. Number 98 was an imposing gray stone structure with a white marble bench running along the length of it. It was just about one o'clock and there was nothing to do but sit and wait.

Beatrice's stomach had taken up residence in her throat. She forced herself to sit still and reread her notes. Marco flopped down beside her, grabbed her guide-book, and flipped through it lazily.

Every time a car or scooter approached, Beatrice held her breath. She eyeballed every person who walked down the street, imagining each as the thief's secret contact. A businessman, briefcase in hand, barking into a cell phone. A pair of tall blond tourists snapping photos at every other step. A teenage couple, their arms wrapped around each other's waists. But no one stopped or did anything suspicious—unfortunately.

She fanned herself with her notebook. It was the middle of the day, and there was no shade on either side of the street. She could feel her freckles multiplying. By one-thirty, her nerves were at a breaking point. She was hot, sweaty, and uncomfortable. Her stomach growled at her for skipping lunch and as the clock ticked closer to two, she worried that their suspect's appointment had been canceled. Or maybe Marco had got the whole thing wrong.

He had put down her guidebook and was doing what Italians do best: chilling out. *La dolce far niente*, her dad called it: sweet idleness. It looked like Marco was a pro, his head leaned back, his eyes closed, and a contented expression on his face.

"How can you be so relaxed at a time like this?" Beatrice burst out.

He slid his eyes toward her under half-closed lids. "I think one stressed-out person is enough for any team, don't you?"

"You're right," she grumbled, smiling inwardly that he thought of them as a team. "Maybe I'm nervous because I'm starving!"

"There's a café down the street. Why don't you get some water and a snack?" Marco suggested. "Grab a water for me too while you're at it."

Beatrice gave him a sideways glance. She didn't want to risk abandoning the stakeout. Still, she could use a drink of water.

"Yeah, okay," she said hesitantly. "I'll be two seconds. Keep your eyes open and shout if anything happens." Marco nodded silently. "Want anything to eat?"

"No, thanks."

Beatrice hurried the block and a half to the café, and paid for two bottles of water and a *panino*. While she waited for it to be wrapped up, she stuck her head out the door and peered down the street to see if she was missing anything.

She gasped.

Marco was talking to someone—a man. She couldn't hear their voices but it looked like they were deep in conversation, gesticulating this way and that.

She headed for the door when a voice rang out. *"Signorina! Il suo panino! La sua acqua!"* [1]

She'd forgotten all about her snack. *"Grazie!"* she breathed, grabbing the paper bag and water bottles. She darted outside and ran back to Marco, who was sitting in the same position as before. The man was gone.

"Who was that?" she demanded breathlessly.

. . . .

1. "Miss! Your sandwich! Your water!"

"Who?" he asked languidly, without lifting his head.

"That man you were talking to just a minute ago!" Was he trying to be difficult, or was it just the heat?

"Oh, him. Just some guy asking for directions."

Beatrice had a niggling feeling he wasn't telling the truth. "Directions to where?" She winced at the sharpness in her voice but couldn't help it.

"To Ponte Sisto. What do you care?"

Before she could protest, a now-familiar scooter buzzed toward them, coming to a stop less than a block away. Beatrice slid back onto the bench, grabbed her guidebook, and pretended to be a clueless tourist.

After jerking his scooter onto its kickstand, the gangly thief walked up to the door less than two feet from her. He studied the list of names on the shiny brass intercom and pressed a button. Beatrice's heart pounded and it took a will of iron not to look up. She unfolded her map instead and sat quivering behind it.

"*Chi è?*"[2] squawked a high-pitched voice from the intercom.

. . . .

2.   "Who is it?"

"*Sono io, Luca,*"[3] he said in low tones.

"*Ascoltami bene,*"[4] said the other voice. It came harsh and metallic through the tiny brass speaker, yet for all that, it sounded vaguely familiar.

Luca the thief cast a suspicious glance at Beatrice and Marco. Beatrice froze, but Marco acted quickly. "I know you want to see the Vatican, sis, but I want to go to the Colosseum!" He indicated the guidebook, slapping the page for emphasis.

Beatrice immediately picked up his cue. "Oh, please can we go to the Vatican?" she whined. "We can see the Colosseum tomorrow!"

"Excuse me!" Marco looked up at Luca. "Do you speak English? We're a bit lost and need to get to the Colosseum," he said with an exaggerated American accent.

"*No,*" said Luca contemptuously. He turned back to the intercom. "*Dimmi.*"[5]

The exchange was brief, but Beatrice couldn't follow a single word. Even had she been able to understand

<hr />

3. "It's me, Luca."
4. "Listen carefully."
5. "Tell me."

Italian, the voice from the intercom was garbled and tinny. She could only hope that Marco was getting everything.

When the conversation was over, Beatrice and Marco kept up their fake argument as Luca hopped on his scooter and sped away. When he was out of sight, Beatrice turned to Marco expectantly.

"Well? What did they say?" she asked, with a minuscule prick of suspicion. Would Marco tell her the truth? Was he hiding something? She dismissed the thoughts as silly. He wanted to save the fountain as much as she did.

"Come on, let's get out of here." He tugged her arm and they turned their steps toward the Ghetto. After walking in silence for a minute or two, Beatrice could stand the suspense no longer. "Tell me what's going on!" she burst out. She felt the language barrier more strongly than ever, and vowed to study Italian harder.

"The woman on the intercom gave Luca another appointment, for tomorrow night, at midnight."

"Did she say where?"

"No, but she told him to deliver the 'merchandise' to the Frenchman."

"The merchandise?" Beatrice yelped. "You think he meant the turtles?"

"Well, they didn't actually say the word, but that's what it sounded like."

"Then that means they'll be handed over tomorrow! We've got to stop them!"

"I know! We can hide somewhere nearby and wait for him to remove the turtles from the fountain."

Beatrice stopped in her tracks. "What are you talking about?"

"Isn't it obvious? Luca's going to steal the turtles tomorrow night!"

Beatrice let out a frustrated breath. "I'm telling you, he *already* stole them, on Monday night—I saw it. He replaced them with replicas, and the *real* turtles are stashed away somewhere. If my intuition is correct, they're in Caterina's secret room, in the ruins under the Mattei Palace."

Marco shot her a patronizing look. "First of all, you don't solve crimes with intuition, you solve them with *facts*. And second, there've been too many coincidences; it just isn't plausible."

"What coincidences?"

"Like you getting into the palace, seeing Caterina's

portrait, just *happening* to find her diary? I'm sorry, but it seems a bit far-fetched."

His words were like a punch in the gut. "You think I'm making it all up?"

"Of course not, but I just don't see what the theft of the turtles has to do with the diary or that secret room. You're making all these connections with no evidence to back them up. And even if you're right, how would we get down there? You said yourself the ruins are closed to the public."

"I didn't say it would be easy," Beatrice muttered. She smarted at his cynical words, but was he right to doubt her? Was she putting too much stock in hunches?

They made their way down Via Giulia in silence. At the end of the street, the Tiber River greeted them. They gazed into its murky waters as if it held the answers they needed.

Beatrice broke the silence. "I read in one of my dad's books that Palazzo Giacomo Mattei is part of a larger structure, the Isola Mattei."

"The 'Mattei Island'?" he translated dubiously.

"Four separate palaces that belonged to different branches of the Mattei family," she explained, satisfied she knew something about the Ghetto he didn't. "It takes up an entire city block. Look." She unfolded her map and traced her finger around the streets that bordered Isola Mattei. "Maybe the palaces are connected somehow—if we can get into one of the others, maybe we can find a way into Palazzo Giacomo Mattei," she said, her enthusiasm mounting, "and from there, the ruins and the secret room!"

Marco shrugged. "Sounds like a long shot."

"You have a better idea?" she asked tersely.

"I don't know, Beatrice. I just know there's a lot more to Rome than you'll ever find in some book."

"What's that supposed to mean?"

"You show up a month ago and think you know everything there is to know about the Ghetto."

"And?"

"And, there's no way some *Bostonian* knows my city better than I do."

Something inside Beatrice snapped. She'd had it with his contemptuous attitude and constant skepticism.

"Fine," she hissed. "I'll stop boring you with my ideas since you disagree with all of them. If you won't help me, I'll just do it myself." She snatched her map out of his hand and stormed off without a backward glance.

twenty

SYNCHRONICITY

Beatrice dragged herself home, knee-deep in resentment and frustration. More than ever since her arrival, she felt utterly alone. She thought she'd found a friend in Marco, but all he did was criticize and doubt her.

As she walked the narrow, winding streets, his words clattered around in her head like a defective wind-up toy. *Intuition . . . coincidences . . . long shot . . . far-fetched . . .* One moment she'd been convinced she had it all figured out, but one word of doubt from Marco had her believing she was rushing to improbable conclusions.

Was she silly to think she could trust her intuition?

Or follow a trail of unlikely coincidences? Was she seeing connections that didn't exist?

With these questions stirring in her head, Beatrice's feet led her back to Piazza Mattei and the Turtle Fountain. The bronze boys were still laughing, ignorant of what had been stolen from them. The fake turtles were poised to plop into the upper basin. Someday the city would discover they were imposters, but by that time, Bernini's true sculptures would be long gone. It was up to her, she realized with a lurch of responsibility. She alone held the pieces to this puzzle.

She took a deep breath. "I'll find your turtles, if it's the last thing I do!" she vowed, staring up at the sculpted boys. With renewed purpose, she ran up the stairs of her building, taking them two at a time. As she reached the top floor, Signora Costaguti was exiting the rickety elevator under her helmet of white hair. Her arms were full of groceries and her tiny dog yapped at her feet.

"Let me help you!" Beatrice offered. The prim old lady gratefully handed over the groceries and unlocked her door with a trembling hand.

"*Grazie, cara.*" The door swung open with a creak. She held it for Beatrice, who hovered on the threshold.

"Come in, come in, the kitchen is this way."

Beatrice stepped inside and followed Signora Costaguti through the labyrinthine apartment. It could easily have doubled for an antique shop, with old-fashioned furniture, black-and-white photographs in silver frames, and porcelain figurines sitting on spindly-legged tables. Lining the walls were books, books, and more books—even more than her dad had back in Boston. Only the kitchen was modern, and Beatrice lugged the grocery bags inside and set them on the counter.

"Well, here you go," she said. She shifted from one foot to the other, looking for a polite way to make her exit.

"Please, stay and have some iced tea," Signora Costaguti offered. When Beatrice hesitated she added, "I insist."

Beatrice had a feeling she meant it. She obeyed the old lady's instructions to wait in the *salone*. The sofa was upholstered in powder blue velvet, with a straight back and fussy curlicue legs. It was every bit as uncomfortable as it looked. Beatrice's eyes roamed the room, noticing what looked like important works of art. Maybe Signora Costaguti would be at the Mattei auction on Sunday—she clearly liked old stuff.

On the polished coffee table sat a pair of wire-rimmed reading glasses and a newspaper, open to a section titled *Arte e cultura*. She picked up the paper and gave it a cursory glance. *"Capolavoro rubato!"* read the headline. *"L'Abbandonata di Botticelli sparisce dalla collezione Rospigliosi."* Only two of those words held any meaning for Beatrice—Botticelli and Rospigliosi. But they were enough.

As Beatrice stared at the article in vain, Signora Costaguti appeared holding a silver tray with a crystal jug of iced tea and two matching tumblers.

"Such dreadful news!" the *signora* clucked, glancing at the paper. "Another priceless work of art, this time a Botticelli, stolen! And the authorities are *useless!*"

"Another work of art?"

"Yes, that's twice in as many weeks. An ancient cameo depicting Hercules was stolen from the Santarelli collection not ten days ago!" She poured the tea while Beatrice digested this latest morsel of information. One stolen work might have been unconnected to the turtles. But two?

Signora Costaguti arranged herself in an armchair

like an ailing queen and took a dainty sip of tea. Despite her age—she looked at least ninety—she was still a striking woman. She had high cheekbones, a swan-like neck, and piercing blue eyes. She seemed proud, but in a good way, like she'd spent her life doing what she loved, and doing it well. Still, there was something unsettling about her. Her eyes gleamed as if she grasped far more than you were telling her.

"Well, go ahead," the old lady said abruptly. "Drink your tea. You look thirsty."

She was right. After Beatrice's long walk in the midday sun, she was parched and light-headed. She lifted the glass to her lips and drank deeply. The lemony liquid cooled her from the inside out.

"You seem like a clever girl." Signora Costaguti fixed Beatrice with her penetrating glare. "Now, tell me, just what have you been investigating?"

Beatrice felt like she'd been tossed into a tub of ice water. What did she know? *How* did she know it?

"Signora Costaguti, I don't—"

"Please." She held up a hand, white and speckled as a quail's egg. "Call me Mirella. You might as well tell me what you've been up to. It's useless to deny it; I've seen you prowling around."

Beatrice's mouth went dry. Was she threatening her or just being a busybody?

"Go on." Mirella stared her down.

Beatrice wasn't about to reveal her secrets, but maybe she could tell her a half-truth?

"Well," she hesitated, "I've been . . . *researching* some of the art and history of the neighborhood, just to, you know, keep myself busy. And I've discovered some unbelievable things."

"What sort of *unbelievable* things?"

"Oh, I don't know, the fact that the turtles on the fountain are the work of Bernini, that under the palace across the square are ruins of an ancient theater . . ."

"That's not unbelievable, my child—that's Rome! There's an entire ancient city down there; everything is built on top of *something*. And as for Bernini, there's scarcely a piazza or church in this city that doesn't contain one of his masterpieces."

Beatrice mulled this over. "Yeah, that must be it. Everything in Rome seems to have some crazy history. Every time I think I understand something, the reality is a thousand times more complicated than I'd imagined—and goes back a thousand more years."

"In Rome, past and present are inextricably linked. This city has seen three thousand years of human existence, three thousand years of love and war, life and death, joy and despair. That kind of past leaves its mark on a city. Every building has a story behind it, every piazza has memories, every work of art was influenced by an older one. *Everything* is connected."

Goose bumps crept up Beatrice's arms as the words seeped into her soul. *Everything is connected.* It was as if Mirella had read her unspoken questions and given her an answer.

Mirella narrowed her eyes shrewdly. "There's something you're not telling me."

Beatrice sat silently, deciding how much to reveal. "Well, you see," she said, choosing her words carefully, "I've been trying to shed some light on a . . . a disappearance—"

"A disappearance? That sounds serious."

"More of a mix-up, really," she said hastily. "The weird thing is, every time I'm missing some important piece of the puzzle, it just magically appears."

"Magically?"

"I don't mean wizard-type magic, with wands and

spells and stuff. More like strange coincidences that keep pushing me in the right direction. At least, I *hope* it's the right direction."

"For example?" Mirella sat even straighter, if that were possible.

"Well, the other day I was looking for some very specific information, and I just happened to find this . . . this *book* that told me everything I needed to know. And I keep meeting people who know all about the subject I'm researching. And I know it sounds crazy, but I saw this painting and I felt like it was . . . communicating with me somehow." She looked down, afraid she'd said too much. "It's as if, everywhere I turn, whatever I'm looking for pops up right under my nose, even when I didn't know I was looking for it."

For a long moment Mirella said nothing, but sat perfectly still with fire in her eyes. Finally she spoke. "What you are experiencing is synchronicity, *cara mia*."

"Synchronicity?" Beatrice liked the way the word felt in her mouth, the crunch of the consonants as they bumped up against each other, the way each syllable danced across her tongue. Whatever it meant, it had to be something wonderful.

"Synchronicity is the theory of meaningful coincidence."

Meaningful coincidence. The words didn't seem to go together.

"According to the theory of synchronicity," Mirella said, "nothing happens entirely by chance. When you focus on something with enough intensity, with enough clarity of purpose, in your small way, you participate in the creative process of the universe. Events intermesh, opportunities present themselves, people who have the means to help you are thrown into your path, all bringing you toward your goal.

"Such as you running into me, for instance," she continued. "You think it was just a coincidence? Let me ask you, what were you doing just before we met on the landing?"

Beatrice thought for a moment. "I'd been feeling really doubtful about this . . . this project I'm working on, and was on the point of giving up actually. Then I realized I just had to keep going. I *have* to get to the bottom of this."

"*Vedi?* You see? You made a commitment, and the universe acknowledged it. Think back to all the other times you noticed these *strange coincidences* as you call them. You'll find they are not coincidences at all, but the responses of an invisible force prodding you along."

A world of possibility opened before Beatrice. Still, her skeptical side told her it was too good to be true. "How does it work?"

"Don't worry about *how*. Not yet anyway. For now, just be aware. Pay attention to what is all around you, and you'll feel the universe synchronize with your own consciousness."

"Do a lot of people know about synchronicity?"

"Surprisingly few considering the theory was introduced by Carl Jung in the 1920s. Many scientists dismiss it, perhaps because they've never experienced it for themselves, or refuse to recognize it when it does occur. They believe it has no basis in science. But remember this: just because something cannot be proved, that doesn't mean it does not exist."

Beatrice stood up suddenly, knocking her knees against the coffee table. A fire had been lit in her belly and she didn't have a moment to lose.

"Thank you so much for the tea, and for . . . everything," she breathed. "I really should be going, though."

Mirella wore the knowing smile of someone who'd lived long and seen much. She escorted Beatrice to the door, then took hold of her arm, fixing her once more with her piercing gaze. *"Beatrice."* She said it the Italian way. "Synchronicity will point you in the right direction, but the rest is up to you."

twenty-one

A MISSING MAP

Synchronicity. She could hardly believe there was a word for what she'd been experiencing. Mirella's words echoed in her head: *Everything is connected.* She'd known the legend was connected to the theft of the turtles; she'd felt it in her bones. Now she didn't have to doubt herself anymore, no matter what Marco said. Especially now that she knew two other works of art had been stolen, not to mention the break-in at the academy. Whoever was behind these robberies was after more than just Bernini's turtles. Who knew how many masterpieces he'd get his hands on before he was stopped?

Back in her room, she dug out the translation of the diary and reread every passage, looking for clues she might have missed. Eventually she came upon an entry she'd skipped before, and it made her heart stop.

3 February 1600

Today I found, among the many treasures here in my secret room, a chest full of documents that must have belonged to Muzio's grandfather. Most are of little interest to me and I left them where they were, but one I couldn't help keeping for myself. It seems the old duke made a map of these underground chambers, plotting out exactly how to get from the library to his secret room. If only I'd had it before! It would have saved me hours of searching and more than a little fear.

Of course, I don't need it now—I've memorized the route down to the very last step. Nevertheless, I keep it tucked in my diary at all times, another irresistible secret.

How had she missed this before, and why hadn't Marco mentioned it? There existed a map that showed the way to the secret room, and—Beatrice reread the last sentence with disbelief—Caterina had kept it in her *diary*?

She ran to her wardrobe, where she'd stashed the original diary. She leafed through every page, looked for hidden pockets, and even gently shook it by its spine, but there was nothing there but words.

Marco! Had he taken it? A wave of nausea rose from her stomach. Had he been in on this from the start? Her mind invented a dozen scenarios of how Marco might be involved in the theft of the turtles.

But something in the back of her mind was poking her, saying, *If Marco's in on it, why did he give you back the diary? Why didn't he just keep if for himself?*

Because he didn't want me to get suspicious! she answered back.

Then why did he translate the part of the diary that mentions the secret room and the map? Wouldn't he have left those parts out if he were deceiving you?

The inner voice made one last attempt to defend her friend. *Maybe the map wasn't in the diary at all. Maybe it was lost centuries ago.*

Beatrice ignored this last internal comment. As far as she was concerned, Marco was up to something. It all made sense now. She mulled over the signs she'd so foolishly ignored: how he'd urged her to lend him the diary, the information he knew about the Mattei family, the man he'd been talking to secretly on Via Giulia. And come to think of it, wasn't it Marco who'd suggested she go get a snack? Had he had an appointment to meet someone there as well? Was he warning the thief not to give anything away?

She shook her head ruefully. She'd been so excited to have a friend, someone to share her adventure with, that she hadn't taken the time to get to know him, to find out if she could trust him.

But what exactly was he up to? She paced the length of her room, imagining possible explanations. He wasn't connected with the Mattei family, that much was obvious. Maybe he wanted to steal the turtles for himself? She thought of his father's antique shop—those turtles would net a fortune!

Her head spun. She went to the window and leaned out, gulping down air, finally cooler now that the sun had set. Staring down at the fountain, she remembered the silly vow she'd made just hours before. What made her, a thirteen-year-old girl in a foreign country, think she could solve a crime on her own? There was only one word for the whole situation: hopeless.

When her father arrived an hour later, he found Beatrice lying facedown on her bed.

"What's the matter, sweet pea?"

"Nothing," she groaned into her pillow.

"I wouldn't have pegged you for someone who wallows for nothing," he said, easing her upright. "What have you been up to all week? You've been so preoccupied."

"Nothing."

"'Nothing, nothing . . . ,'" he mimicked. "Why won't you talk to me? I thought we were a team."

A sudden stab of guilt was followed closely by a burn of resentment. How many times had she tried to share her adventure with him? Explain what she was up to? Ask for advice? And every time he'd been too busy to listen, or worse, scoffed at her for being silly.

"Come on," he insisted, "tell me what's bothering you."

"I'm just homesick," she mumbled. At least that was part of the truth.

"Well, that's normal. It takes time to get used to a new city, not to mention a new country. You'll get the hang of it!" He rumpled her hair and she managed a weak smile. "Oh, I almost forgot; I have a little surprise for you."

"Really? What is it?" Her spirits buoyed in spite of herself.

"Did you know that your Italian teacher is also an art history student?"

"No." What could that possibly have to do with a surprise?

"Well, tomorrow morning I have to spend a few hours in the library, and Ginevra has agreed to take you on a cultural outing! You're going to visit Palazzo Farnese, a Renaissance palace designed by Michelangelo."

Beatrice's face fell.

"What? I thought you'd be excited to do a little culturing."

"I am, but . . ."

"But what?"

"I haven't seen you all week, that's what." She glared at him, trying to look more angry than hurt. "Tomorrow's Saturday; I thought we'd spend the day together." She bit her lower lip to keep it from quivering.

"Ah, my own little Bea," her father said tenderly, enfolding her in his arms. "And here I thought you were fed up with your old man's company."

She buried her head in his chest, her resentment evaporating. He smelled reassuringly familiar, a combination of aftershave, typewriter ribbons, and dusty old books. She wanted to tell him how alone she felt, how out of place and out of her depth. How much she still needed him. But her voice stuck in her throat.

"Listen." He took hold of her shoulders. "You know how important my research is. I've got to get in as much work as I can before the library closes for August. After that, I'm all yours. I promise," he added with a wink. "You'll have a great time tomorrow. I've heard that palace is just dripping with art. And you like Ginevra, don't you?"

"Sure." She shrugged. "She's nice, I guess."

"She seems like a bright young woman. She's charging me an arm and a leg, but I suppose she's worth it. She'll certainly be able to tell you a lot more about the palace than I could."

"You mean you *don't* know everything?" Beatrice teased, her eyes wide with mock astonishment.

"Believe it or not, there are one or two subjects your otherwise omniscient father hasn't *fully* mastered," he humbly conceded.

Her left eyebrow rose. "Only one or two?"

"Maximum three. Just promise you won't tell my students."

Beatrice smirked. "I guess I *have* to go then, so I'll be able to teach *you* a few things."

Especially, she added silently, *since my investigation is turning into a big, fat flop.*

twenty-two

AT THE FRENCH EMBASSY

If Beatrice had been impressed by Palazzo Giacomo Mattei, she hadn't seen anything yet. As she and Ginevra swept up the grand staircase of Palazzo Farnese, practically as wide as it was long, Beatrice's eyes bugged with wonder.

"This place is huge," she said, "and practically empty!" There wasn't a guidebook-toting tourist in sight, only suit-clad professional types.

"Thees ees the seat of the French embassy, and the public are never allowed open access to an embassy, no matter how artistically important the palace ees."

"Then how did *we* get in?"

"Let us say . . . I know people. In Italy, you cannot do anything without . . ." She paused, as if searching for the right word. ". . . *connections*."

And in fact, when they had approached the behemoth palace, a hulking cube of stone that dwarfed every other building in sight, Ginevra had given her name to a pair of police officers stationed at the front doors. They had consulted a clipboard and waved them inside.

Beatrice wandered from room to opulent room, feeding her pupils on marble sculptures, trompe l'oeil ceilings, ancient artifacts, and a seemingly endless number of frescoes.

"I can't believe all this belonged to a single family!"

Ginevra sneered. "The Farnese family were obscenely wealthy. They had more money than they knew what to do with, more money than God. They even tried to build a private bridge across the river, connecting this palace to their villa on the other side!" She snorted with contempt. "Reech people always theenk they are better than everyone else," she added under her breath.

Every so often, Ginevra stopped in front of a work of art and rattled off an explanation about the artist's style, the subject of the work, or the history of the Farnese family. It wasn't that Beatrice wasn't interested. Ordinarily she'd have relished having an expert all to herself to describe what she was seeing, to make the art come alive.

But she couldn't help it; her mind kept flitting back to the turtles. She sneaked a peek at her watch. It was almost one o'clock: in just eleven hours, the turtles would be in Cambriolage's hands. They'd be as good as gone. But what was *she* supposed to do to stop it?

If only she had Caterina's map. The moment that thought darted into her brain, Marco's betrayal pierced her afresh. She'd pushed the memory down into the crannies of her mind, but here it was, bobbing back up like a cork, reminding her she no longer had a partner in this daunting task. She tried, without success, to kick the thought away.

They ambled into a massive barrel-vaulted gallery with frescoes on every inch of the walls and ceiling. In spite of her swirling thoughts, Beatrice was dumbstruck. Her eyes didn't know where to look first.

"Ah, *eccoci*, here we are," Ginevra said. "The galleria of Annibale Carracci: the masterpeece of the palace."

Ginevra narrated the complicated myths, featuring pagan gods Beatrice was vaguely familiar with—Jupiter, Juno, Venus, Bacchus—depicted in the frescoes. As Ginevra spoke, stories of love, courage, and victory exploded into life before Beatrice's eyes.

But after a good twenty minutes, the nervous tickling in her belly returned. It was all well and good to try to distract herself with art, but the hour of truth was ticking closer.

As they continued through the last few rooms of their tour, none so impressive as the galleria, Beatrice tuned out her teacher's melodic voice and let her mind wander. If the turtles were being handed over to Cambriolage tonight, they'd have to be taken from their hiding place in the Mattei Palace. If she were going to have a chance of stopping it, she had to be there.

"Beatrice?"

But how in the world was she supposed to sneak into a private palace on her own?

"Beatrice??"

It wasn't as if she could just walk up to the front door and ring the bell.

"Beatrice!"

She spun around. She was so caught up in her thoughts that she'd failed to recognize the Italian version of her name.

"Sorry," she said sheepishly, "I must've zoned out. You know, looking at all the art."

Ginevra glared in disapproval, but the spark of mischief that danced in her black eyes convinced Beatrice she wasn't as angry as she pretended to be. Suddenly the answer was clear—it was standing right in front of her. Ginevra *knew people*. She had *connections*; she'd said so herself. If she'd had no problem getting into the French embassy, a palace that was about to be auctioned off would probably be a piece of cake.

Beatrice had been reluctant to let any adults in on her investigations, but what choice did she have? If she couldn't find a way inside the palace, the turtles would be lost forever. And with those mischievous eyes lurking behind a severe facade, Ginevra looked like a person who'd relish an adventure. Not to mention her obvious passion for art. She'd probably *want* to help.

The question was, would Ginevra believe her? Beatrice didn't exactly have any proof, as Marco had helpfully pointed out. She felt another stab at the memory of his mocking tone.

What was it Mirella had said? She could hear the old lady's voice in her head, a whistle cutting through the babble of her muddled thoughts. *Opportunities present themselves, people who have the means to help you are thrown into your path, all bringing you toward your goal . . .*

Beatrice drew in a deep breath, stretching it out as long as she could, as if to give herself time to change her mind. "Ginevra?" she finally ventured.

"*Sì?*" The fake furrow melted off her forehead.

"Well, it's slightly off-topic, but I was wondering . . ."

"Just a moment. I want to show you one more room." Behind Ginevra's green-framed glasses, her eyes brimmed with the promise of a spectacular sight.

They made their way along a wide corridor, hung with heavy tapestries, each one woven with gold and scarlet thread. As they approached a set of carved wooden doors—themselves a work of art—a man in a somber black suit stepped in front of them.

He and Ginevra exchanged a few words in rapid Italian, Ginevra's voice rising slightly in objection. Even though Beatrice didn't understand a word, it was clear that they were being turned away.

"*Peccato.* What a shame," said Ginevra as they headed toward a marble staircase. "I wanted to show you a magneeficent fresco in the ambassador's office, but the ambassador ees inside, so we cannot go een." She clucked with contempt, as if the French ambassador being in his own office was highly inconsiderate.

Beatrice wasn't so sorry. Her eyes were on overload from all the art she'd just gorged on. Besides, she had other things on her mind. Like getting up the nerve to ask Ginevra the big question, wondering how much of her illicit plans she'd have to reveal.

She was steeling her nerve when a tubby, middle-aged man came huffing up the stairs in their direction. He sported a neat gray beard and a smart gray suit, and as he came closer, his gaze fell on Beatrice with a glimmer of recognition.

twenty-three

ENTER JACQUES RAMBEAU

Beatrice's blood froze as she locked eyes with Cambriolage, the man who had ordered the theft of Bernini's turtles—if not for himself, then someone he was working for. The Frenchman's gaze flicked to Ginevra, then back to Beatrice with a look of confusion so fleeting she couldn't be sure if she'd seen or imagined it.

What was he doing here, of all places? On second thought, it *was* the French embassy, and he was French, after all. Maybe it wasn't such a coincidence.

Beatrice couldn't help scowling at the man she knew was involved in a despicable crime against art, but he didn't meet her eye again. On her other side,

Ginevra's head was down, her gaze suddenly riveted to her fingernails. As Monsieur Cambriolage passed them, he pulled his hand out of his pocket and a tiny scrap of paper fluttered to the ground near Beatrice's feet.

Quick as a wink, Beatrice swooped down and scooped up the paper. She crumpled it into her fist and peeked over her shoulder to make sure no one had seen her. Monsieur Cambriolage heaved himself up the last few steps, smoothed his jacket, and strutted up to the ambassador's door.

The stern man who had shooed Beatrice and Ginevra away just moments before flung open the door without waiting to be asked. Beatrice saw a flash of color within—gold, red, black, and green—from a fresco on the wall behind a massive oak desk. A tall, dour-looking man with a bald head appeared behind the door. The two men shook hands.

"*Ah, Cambriolage,*" snarled the bald man, whom Beatrice guessed was none other than the French ambassador. "*Entrez, entrez,*"[1] he said, his voice gruff and scratchy.

. . . .

1. "Come in, come in."

"*Monsieur l'Ambassadeur*," said Cambriolage, jolly and round as a hedgehog by comparison, and disappeared into the office. The ambassador turned to the underling who had opened the door, barked an order at him in French, and slammed the door. Beatrice was thankful she wasn't in *that* meeting.

When she turned back around, Ginevra was at the bottom of the staircase, eyeing her shrewdly. Beatrice scurried down the rest of the steps and met her tutor's penetrating stare with a casual smile.

"Do you know that man?" Ginevra's tone was even but her eyes were sharp as shattered glass.

"N-no," Beatrice stammered, as casually as possible. "I just wanted to get a peek at that fresco you mentioned. Why, do *you* know him?" she countered, forcing her voice to be nonchalant.

"I do not think so . . ." Ginevra said, turning her head, a hint of color spotting her cheeks. "He *does* remind me of one of my former universitee professors . . . but no, I do not theenk it was heem." She shrugged. "*Un attimo.*[2] I need to peek up my *telefonino.*" She pulled a bit of paper out of her handbag and approached a security

• •

2. "One moment."

guard seated behind a counter.

Beatrice opened her hand slyly to reveal the bit of crumpled paper. The tiny white square read *313*. Of course! It was a claim slip, identical to the one Ginevra had just handed over. Electronic devices were strictly forbidden in embassies, and all visitors—even Monsieur Cambriolage—had to leave them behind with the guard.

Ginevra had retrieved her cell phone and was tapping away with furiously flying fingers. With her tutor's attention absorbed, Beatrice silently slid Cambriolage's claim slip across the counter to the guard on duty. She smiled up at him innocently. She'd never been so grateful to be a foreigner than at that moment, not expected to put words to her request. She only hoped the guard didn't have a good memory; whatever object the slip claimed had been deposited mere minutes before.

She held her breath until the guard, without a trace of suspicion, handed her a sleek black smartphone. Smiling her thanks, she stuffed it into her back pocket just as Ginevra looked up.

"Andiamo?"[3]

"Andiamo!"[4] Beatrice replied, with a tad more enthusiasm than the situation called for.

They walked into the blaring sunshine and Ginevra turned to her pupil. "Now, what was eet you wanted to ask me?"

Maybe it was Marco's recent deception, still stinging like a fresh burn, or perhaps the suspicious appearance of Monsieur Cambriolage, or maybe even the stolen cell phone smoldering in her pocket. Whatever it was, it made her hesitate, then come to a decision. She'd gotten herself mixed up in this mystery alone; she was going to solve it alone.

She turned to Ginevra with an innocent shrug. "Must've slipped my mind."

Beatrice's belly spun like a hamster in a wheel, but whether out of fright or glee, she couldn't quite say. She was sure that any second a policeman would grab her by the shoulders and shake her down. But the dread of being caught with someone else's cell phone

. . . .

3. "Shall we go?"
4. "Let's go!"

was outweighed by the anticipation of the clues she might discover.

Once she and Ginevra went their separate ways, Beatrice snuck down a side street and tore the phone out of her pocket. She pressed a button at random and the device flickered on. An image of an empty battery flashed across the screen: only 3 percent power left, it warned.

She quickly tapped on the messaging app. The most recent text came from a certain Jacques Rambeau. She selected it to find a conversation made up of dozens of messages—all in French of course! Why did it seem like every time she was on the verge of a discovery, some foreign language got in her way?

The battery flashed 2 percent just as she reached the last few messages. She was about to give up, her hope deflating, when a familiar word caught her eye: Mattei. Her heart stopped and she scanned the message in question. It consisted of a list, all in French, but even so, she managed to decipher a few words.

Camée d'Hercule—Collection Santarelli
La Délaissée de Botticelli—Collection Rospigliosi
Tortues de Bernini—Piazza Mattei

Miroir à main en bronze étrusque—Académie Américaine

Mangeurs de Haricots de Carracci—Collection Colonna

Putti de Raphael—Académie de Saint-Luc

An invisible ice cube slid down her spine. There could no longer be any doubt. Monsieur Cambriolage wasn't just after Bernini's turtles. Those four sculptures were only the tip of the felonious iceberg, only a fraction of art he was in the process of acquiring—and not in the legal way. The Botticelli had already been stolen, and according to Mirella, so had the Cameo of Hercules. It was only too clear the turtles were next. How long would it take before Cambriolage got his hands on the rest of the items on the list?

Then she did a double take. *Académie Américaine?* That could only mean one thing: the American Academy. Her dad said there'd been a break-in, but they hadn't managed to steal anything. Maybe they'd try again. He'd lose his job and they'd be on the next flight back to Boston. Panic wrapped its bony fingers around her windpipe.

One percent. Any second now the screen would

go black. She clicked on the contact info for Jacques Rambeau. Whoever he was, he was behind these despicable crimes, and she wasn't going to let him get away with it.

The contact page displayed nothing but a phone number. It was a start, at any rate. She scrabbled for her own phone out of habit, only to remember the broken shards of plastic she'd shoved into her nightstand drawer. She clawed blindly in her bag for pen and paper, not taking her eyes off the number. "332-747-8992," she said aloud. "332-747-8992, 332-747-8992 . . ." Just as she got hold of her pen, the screen went black. She scrawled the number on her palm before she had a chance to forget it. She was almost sure she'd got it right. *Almost sure* would have to do.

Now that the phone was useless, she wondered, should she hang on to it? It would make an excellent piece of evidence. But what if it had a tracking device? She imagined a pair of armed thugs showing up on her doorstep in the middle of the night. No, she wasn't about to lead them right to her. Better to take it back. But how? She couldn't exactly saunter up to the embassy's security guard and tell him she'd accidently taken the wrong phone. And what if Cambriolage had finished his meeting by now and had already reported it stolen?

With her stomach churning, she slunk back to Piazza Farnese, trying to look as inconspicuous as was possible for a redheaded American girl in Rome. She waited until the guards outside the embassy were distracted, placed the phone atop one of the wooden barriers, and scampered down a side street, her heart thudding in her throat.

She scoured the nearby streets for a pay phone. There were precious few in the city, since hardly anyone used them anymore, but at last she spotted one, its plastic hood covered with squiggles of graffiti. She scrounged in her pockets for a few coins, inserted them into the slot, and dialed the number with a trembling finger.

As the phone rang, her mind went blank. She hadn't even worked out what to say, not that she could say much of anything—in Italian or French. What did she expect? That Jacques Rambeau would just answer the phone and give himself up? In the end, she didn't have time to worry about it. The other line picked up and a gruff "*Oui?*" barked out of the receiver.

"Uh, *bonjour*," Beatrice sputtered, "*Monsieur Rambeau?*"

"*Qui est-ce?*" came a low, threatening tone that was vaguely familiar. The words were close enough to Italian for her to make out his meaning, an ominous "Who is this?"

Beatrice was silent, suddenly grasping the futility of her plan. She had literally nothing to say. What followed was a barrage of French in a voice growling with anger and suspicion. She closed her eyes, wincing against the unintelligible pummeling of verbal abuse. As she did so, a picture formed in her brain, clear as day: the bald ambassador barking orders at the dark-suited subordinate. She hung up the phone and exhaled deeply.

In a flash she was running straight for the Ghetto. Suddenly she didn't care about her suspicions or the harsh words that had passed between them. In that moment, she had to find Marco.

She reached Via del Portico d'Ottavia out of breath, a stitch in her side. The usually bustling street was eerily quiet. Besides a few ambling tourists, no one was out. All the shops were shuttered, the restaurants closed.

Mr. Morello's shop was as deserted as the rest and Beatrice stomped her feet in frustration. Where *was* everyone? It was Saturday, for goodness' sake.

Then she realized with a crash of disappointment. It was *Saturday*—the Sabbath. Any practicing Jew would be at home or at the synagogue to observe the holy day. No wonder the Ghetto was a ghost town.

Sabbath ended at sundown. Beatrice squinted in the direction of the blinding orb, but it was still high in the sky, and wouldn't go down until after dinnertime. Even if her dad let her out of the house at that hour— which was, let's face it, never going to happen—she didn't know where Marco lived. How would she even find him? And by that time, would it be too late?

twenty-four

A CONCERT IS PROPOSED AND
A DOCUMENT DISCLOSED

"So? How was Palazzo Farnese?" asked her dad when he walked in the door a few hours later. "What did you think of those frescoes by Carracci?"

"Pretty impressive," said Beatrice distractedly.

All in all, it had been a successful mission. But even with this new and devastating information, she still had no feasible plan of how to save the turtles—not to mention the other works on Cambriolage's troubling list.

"Did you learn a lot?"

"Oh, yeah," she said, with more meaning than her

dad could have guessed. "But it would've been more fun if *you'd* been there."

"You're right, sweet pea, I've been neglecting you dreadfully! But I'm going to make it up to you. Tonight."

"Tonight?" Beatrice squeaked.

A grin spread across her father's face. "I got us tickets to a concert!"

"For . . . *tonight.*" It seemed as though Beatrice's good luck was turning.

"The concert starts at eight-thirty. I know it's a bit late, but things happen later in Italy, and anyway, tomorrow's Sunday. We can sleep in."

"What kind of music?" she asked, playing for time as she racked her brain for a believable excuse.

"Classical." He pulled the tickets out of his pocket. "Chopin, Brahms, and Beethoven piano sonatas in the courtyard of Palazzo Mattei di Giove."

"What?" The spinning world screeched to a halt.

"Chopin, Brahms—"

"No, no, the last part. Palazzo . . . ?"

"Palazzo Mattei di Giove."

"That's just across the square!" She didn't add that it was *one of the four palaces that made up Isola Mattei.*

"I know, that's why I got the tickets. I thought it might be fun to explore one of the palaces in the neighborhood, and hear some great music at the same time."

Beatrice couldn't believe her luck—no, it wasn't luck. It was synchronicity: another meaningful coincidence. She had no idea where the night would lead, but she'd better be prepared.

Back in her room, she gathered a few indispensable items, a compact flashlight, a compass, a box of matches, a canvas tote bag, and an empty backpack, and squished them into her roomiest shoulder bag.

She grabbed the floor plan of Isola Mattei that she'd photocopied from her father's book and studied it for the millionth time. In just a few hours she'd be in the courtyard of Palazzo Mattei di Giove, but she needed to get to the palace *next door*. Were the two connected somehow? Was there a way to get from one to the next? The complex diagram offered no obvious solutions.

Dismissing the minor detail of *how* she'd break into the palace, she did have a plan for what to do once she was there. She grabbed Marco's translation of the diary and flipped through it until she found the passage she was looking for.

> *. . . in a part of the library I had*
> *never explored before . . . behind the*
> *globe and an armchair, in the corner, with*
> *very poor light . . . a slender volume of*
> *Aristotle . . . I tugged the book . . .*
> *an entire section of the bookcase shifted.*
> *It was a secret door . . .*

Beatrice's breath came short and quick as she imagined herself discovering the secret passageway. If it really did exist, all she had to do was find the right book, and pull. But then what? Who knew what kind of convoluted maze the passage led to? If only she had the map.

Her gut tightened as she envisioned Marco pocketing it. But was he really capable of such a thing? She ran her finger along a line of his cramped handwriting, grazing the words he had so diligently translated.

Overcome with uncertainty and regret, she threw the notebook aside and flung herself onto her bed. She lay facedown, her head lolling over the side, wondering how she'd ever be able to thwart this crime all on her own. Not to mention the ones that were bound to follow.

Her nose wrinkled at the mess lurking under the bed: a pair of mismatched sandals, a stray headband, a piece of folded yellow paper, and the new earphones she thought she'd lost, all keeping company with a litter of dust bunnies. She reached for her earphones, nearly toppling off the bed. As she pulled at the cord, one of the earbuds caught the edge of the folded paper, dragging it from under the bed.

It looked enticingly ancient, with peeling edges and as many wrinkles as the back of Mirella's hand. Beatrice snatched the yellowing parchment and blew off the dust. She unfolded it incredulously, holding her breath, not daring to hope that it could possibly be the thing she needed most. But as soon as the aged document lay open before her, she knew without a doubt it was the map to Caterina's secret room.

But where had it come from? And what had it been doing under *her* bed?

She recalled the night she'd fallen asleep while reading the diary, and woken up to find it open on the floor. Had the map slipped out and blown under the bed?

She slid onto the floor and spread it out with trembling hands.

The lines were faded but she could still make out the fan-shaped diagram of an ancient theater, just like the one in her guidebook only a hundred times more detailed. As she studied the distinctive half-moon shape, an image flashed into her mind: an old-fashioned mahogany desk littered with papers, a diagram like this one sitting right on top. The image staring up at her, as far as she could remember, was identical to the one she'd seen in the Mattei library. A gush of vindication flooded her and she bent down to take a closer look.

The stage ran vertically along the right side, and the seating area—the cavea—curved out to the left. The splayed lines that echoed the rounded shape of the cavea were clearly foundation walls, but she couldn't begin to make sense of the rest of the markings.

She followed the sweeping arc of the cavea with her fingertip, searching for clues. Shaky markings, so faded they were barely discernible, led from a hand-drawn staircase, around a corner, and straight between two of the cavea's foundation walls. There, scratched ever so faintly, was an unmistakable X.

Victory bubbled up within her, but just as quickly it fizzled, like a can of soda suddenly gone flat. Marco.

Her stomach twisted with guilt for assuming he'd stolen the map. Now she didn't know what to think. She'd convinced herself he was planning to betray her, to steal the turtles for himself. It all seemed a bit far-fetched.

She couldn't help wishing he were with her now, puzzling over the map and scheming to get inside the palace. She gazed out the window over the rosy roof tiles that stretched into the distance. The Sabbath sun was setting on the Ghetto, but as to which rooftop was sheltering Marco, it was as much a mystery as the fate of Bernini's turtles.

twenty-five

BRAHMS, BEETHOVEN, AND
A BUSINESS CALL

Stars glinted over the courtyard of Palazzo Mattei di Giove and a lemon-wedge moon slipped behind the wisp of a cloud. Along the pale yellow walls stood dozens of statues, some headless, some armless, keeping watch like wounded sentinels. Marble busts peeked out of niches on the upper level, and the arches of a loggia soared above them.

The heat of the day, which had lingered long past sundown, was abated by a gentle breeze that carried with it the scent of wild jasmine. Elegant women with bare shoulders and tanned men in linen shirts chatted happily. Everyone seemed without a care in the world, with nothing on their minds but the evening's entertainment and the long weeks of late summer ahead.

Everyone but Beatrice.

She sat beside her father in the fifth row wearing a red cotton dress with white polka dots. She'd chosen it for its most convenient feature: pockets. Her foot tapped distractedly and she clutched the straps of her bag to keep her hands from shaking. Inside was everything she needed to recapture Bernini's turtles— everything except a plan.

"You see those ancient sculptures?" her father whispered, making her jump. "If any of them were back home, they'd be locked up in a museum, but here in Rome, they're just—everywhere." His eyes wandered up the walls of the courtyard. "Who do you suppose brought them here?"

"Asdrubale Mattei." The words jumped out of her mouth before she could stop them.

"Who?" he said, and his jaw dropped open.

"Um, you know," she said hurriedly, "the guy who built this palace at the beginning of the 1600s? Come on, Dad, *everyone* knows that."

"No, my little bookworm, I'd wager you're the

only person in this entire audience who knows that! So *that's* what you've been doing locked up in your room every night: studying the history of the neighborhood?"

"Mm-hm," she murmured innocently. The lights went down just in time to hide the blush spreading across her cheeks as the pianist strode toward the inky-black concert grand.

As the melancholy chords of the Chopin ballade filled the courtyard, Beatrice fidgeted in her seat. A glance at her watch showed it was after nine. Less than three hours until the moment of truth. She had to come up with a plan, fast.

Her eyes darted around, scoping out the landscape. Near the entrance of the courtyard, a wide marble staircase led up to the loggia on the floor above. If she could get up there, maybe she could find a way into the adjacent palace. But what about her dad? She couldn't exactly ditch him.

Her thoughts began to swirl and soon she'd lost all track of time. A burst of applause jolted her back to the present and she clapped furiously.

"Would you do me the honor of accompanying

me for a refreshment, *signorina?*" asked her father with exaggerated gallantry as the lights came up for intermission.

They wandered toward the refreshment table, Beatrice's eyes taking in every detail of their surroundings. By the time they reached the table, there was already a cluster of people lined up for snacks.

This was it. Intermission was her only chance. If she was going to do something, she had to do it now. Her eyes shifted from left to right, trying to decide on the best plan of attack. Just as she and her dad reached the front of the line, her dad's cell phone rang.

"Excuse me a moment, sweet pea. I've got to take this."

Typical, Beatrice thought, rolling her eyes, as her dad stepped away from the crowd. Taking advantage of his momentary absence, she racked her brain for a scheme. What if she told him she had to use the ladies' room, and sneaked upstairs instead? Then she could—

"Beatrice, I'm sorry, but we have to go," he said brusquely, his face whiter than usual.

"What? But the concert's not over yet!"

"I know, but this is an emergency. There's been another break-in at the academy. This time a priceless artifact is missing—a nearly three-thousand-year-old bronze hand mirror! I have to go at once."

Beatrice's heart sank. So Cambriolage had gotten his hands on one of the academy's ancient artifacts. Her dad would be fired before he'd even begun teaching and they'd be on the next plane out of there. This wasn't just about the turtles anymore.

Her determination turned fierce. "Dad, we can't go," she stated, trying to temper the panic in her voice. "We'll miss the Beethoven!"

"There's no discussion. Get your things—we're leaving *now*." She knew that tone of voice. It was the same tone he'd used to order her back to bed the night the turtles were stolen. The one he'd used to tell her they were moving to Rome. It was his no-arguing voice.

"I'll drop you off at home and head straight to the academy." He glanced at his wristwatch. "With any luck I'll be back before dawn."

"Dad, you go. Let me stay, please? Beethoven is my favorite!" If only she could explain that this ancient mirror was only one of a long list of artworks that were destined to disappear, and how she alone had a chance to prevent it.

"By yourself? Out of the question!"

"Dad, we live right across the square," she said slowly, keeping her voice as calm as possible. "When the concert's over, I'll be home in less than one minute. You've let me wander all over the neighborhood alone, and I've been fine so far, haven't I?"

"Yes, during the day. By the time the concert ends it'll be nearly eleven!"

"You said yourself everything happens later here. The piazza will be full of people, coming out of the concert, taking an evening stroll. It's a Saturday night in summer!"

"I don't know, Beatrice. You're too young to be out alone at this hour."

"I'm nearly fourteen years old. You've got to let me grow up sometime!"

She saw his determination falter and knew she had won.

"All right," he relented. "But you're to go home immediately after the concert."

"Thank you, Dad!" She threw her arms around him.

He was all business. "Do you have your keys? Your phone?"

"Of course," she said with a twang of guilt. She had one of the two, anyway.

"Make sure no one follows you into the building, and lock the door behind you."

"Dad, I've been home alone at night before."

"Not in Rome. You be careful, Beatrice."

"I will."

He kissed her on the top of the head and hurried out of the courtyard.

"It's now or never," she whispered to no one but herself.

The concertgoers were milling about, drinking prosecco, and chatting happily. It was a lazy Saturday night, the eve of August holidays, and no one was paying attention to the thirteen-year-old redhead slipping behind the wooden barricade and scurrying up the wide marble staircase.

twenty-six

INTRUDER

At the top of the staircase, an intricate iron gate was mercifully propped open. Beatrice squeezed through and stepped onto the loggia. She peered over the railing into the courtyard below, where intermission was still in full swing. No one had noticed her.

A set of open French doors led into a bright room with fancy furniture, a large gilt-framed mirror, and an elaborate chandelier. A gold-colored couch sat in the center of the room with a man's jacket strewn across it. A stack of sheet music and a bottle of water sat on a nearby table and a pair of men's shoes and a garment bag lay scattered on the floor.

Beatrice realized she was standing in the pianist's makeshift dressing room. But it was still intermission; surely he was up here somewhere.

At that precise moment, she heard a toilet flush, followed by firm footsteps coming down the hallway. She had just enough time to duck behind an armchair in the corner of the room. She peeked around the side as the swarthy musician strode into the room. He took a swig from the water bottle, adjusted his bow tie, and checked his appearance in the mirror. After slipping on his shoes and his suit jacket, he stepped onto the loggia and disappeared down the stairs just as Beatrice's heart was getting ready to burst. This was it. She now had the second half of the concert to find her way from this Mattei palace to the one next door.

She waited a few seconds to make sure she was alone, and then crawled out from behind the armchair. Despite the thumping in her chest, she forced herself to do things methodically. She pulled out the photocopy of the Isola Mattei floor plan. By tracing her finger from the palace entrance into the courtyard and up the staircase, she was able to determine her general location. She checked her compass and headed down the hallway in the direction of the neighboring palace.

As she tiptoed down the dark corridor, the plaintive notes of the Beethoven sonata spilled in from the courtyard like raindrops pattering on a rooftop. The palace was eerily empty and she shivered, despite the balmy temperature outside.

Everywhere she turned she met closed doors. The first three she tried were locked solid, with modern locks that would be impossible to pick, even if she knew how. Finally a door handle gave. Her excitement deflated as she stared into a tiny bathroom with no windows.

She soldiered on. Around a corner, the corridor opened onto a wide room with a gilded stucco ceiling and richly paneled walls. Had it once been a ballroom or a formal dining room? Not anymore. In the center sat a vast conference table surrounded by a dozen black leather chairs.

She crossed the room and continued into another corridor. Walking its entire length, she found no sign of a passage to the neighboring palace, just a sweeping staircase up to the higher floor. Time was running out. Soon the concert would be over and they'd be locking up the palace. If she didn't hurry, she'd be locked up in it.

Careful to keep track of her bearings, she ventured up the staircase. More closed doors. More *locked* doors. What now? She couldn't keep going up and up.

Around a corner she came to a few windows. Peering out, she looked down at the roof of the adjacent building—the roof of Palazzo Giacomo Mattei! It was short and inconsequential compared to the palace she was in. Just past the roof was a dark courtyard, the one she'd passed through with Monsieur Cambriolage on her way to the auction viewing, she realized with a jolt.

She flipped the lock of one of the windows and it opened easily. She stuck her head out and tried to gauge how far down the rooftop was. Four feet? Maybe five? She'd always been afraid of heights, and now was no exception. Looking past the roof below at the steep drop into the courtyard beyond made her stomach lurch. No, thank you, she wasn't *that* nuts.

Just as she was about to slam the window shut, the sound of heavy steps rang out from around the corner. Someone—no, two someones by the sound of it—were climbing up the stairs in her direction. Were they just closing the palace for the night, or had someone seen her sneaking in? She decided not to wait and find out.

Before she had time to change her mind, she tossed her bag out the window. It landed with a *plop* on the rooftop below. She lifted one leg over the sill, then the other, said a silent prayer, and hopped down.

Smack!

The rooftop was farther down than it had looked. It wasn't completely flat either. It tilted downward slightly toward the courtyard, but not so much that she couldn't stand upright. The terra-cotta tiles shifted under her as she struggled to keep her balance.

She stood with her arms akimbo, her heart pounding like a warning drum. She tried not to panic, plotting her next move, when suddenly the roof tiles slipped from beneath her feet. Before she had time to blink, she was lying flat on her face. To her relief, the roof wasn't steep at all, perhaps a twenty-degree angle at most. Figuring the damage had already been done, she grabbed the straps of her bag and squirmed down the roof until her feet hit the gutter.

Lying facedown on the rooftop didn't exactly afford her a helpful view. She craned her head over her left shoulder and could just make out a staircase leading from the courtyard up to the piano nobile, the palace's luxurious second floor. Her stomach careened and her head spun, but she forced herself to ignore it.

From what she could tell, the staircase led to directly below the section of roof she was lying on. She closed her eyes and tried to picture the courtyard from the ground, as she'd seen it just a few days before. Did it have a loggia like the one next door? She thought so, but couldn't be sure. She'd have to risk it.

To her right, a drainpipe was attached to the wall at the corner of the courtyard. She inched toward it, and with courage she didn't know she had, she slid her lower body over the edge of the roof. She reached for the copper pipe with her right hand and foot, praying it wouldn't detach and fall straight to the ground. The pipe held and her feet scrabbled for a resting place on top of a nearby window. From there she scampered onto the balustrade of the loggia that was—just as she'd hoped—directly under the roof she'd been clutching on to moments ago.

She hopped onto the floor of the loggia, and raced down the stairs until she was safely on the ground. She would've knelt down and kissed the cobblestones had she not been in such a hurry.

Bong!

Beatrice froze.

Bong!

A nearby church bell was tolling ten o'clock.

Bong!

Only two hours left.

The courtyard was dark and empty. The ground-floor windows were barred and the main door of the palace was—not surprisingly—sealed tight. She had no choice but to head back up the stairs. The French doors opening onto the loggia were soundly locked as well, and Beatrice was running out of options. She tried each window in turn, until at last, one yielded.

Just as she was about to climb inside, a new thought struck her: what if someone was home? According to Monsieur Cambriolage, the Mattei family still lived in the palace—at least until the auction tomorrow. What would they do if they found her sneaking around? Her stomach flip-flopped at the thought.

She peeked in hesitantly, but all was darkness. She slipped through the window as quietly as she could and, once inside, eased it shut. Crouched on the floor, she strained to hear if anyone was about.

Silence.

Stealthy as a cat, Beatrice crept down the hallway, straining to see in the dark. After turning a few blind corners, she reached the grand hall, spooky and still as a deserted train station. She wandered from room to shadowy room, eventually stepping into the picture gallery where the light of a streetlamp filtered through half-shaded windows, casting a hazy glow on the paintings.

Pulled as if by a magnet, she found herself face-to-face with the duchess's portrait. The grimy painting was almost indiscernible in the gloom. And yet, as if lit from within, Caterina's eyes shone out. Having read her most intimate thoughts, Beatrice saw the duchess as more real than ever, as if she could have pulled back the frame to find her standing there behind the wall. A chill like a drop from an icicle ran down her spine as an impalpable communication passed between them. *Go on*, said Caterina's eyes. *Stop them . . . Only you can.*

Beatrice tore her eyes away from the portrait and propelled her body toward the library. When she finally located it, the door was firmly shut. She placed her hand on the big brass knob. Just as she was about to turn it, she heard muffled voices within.

Her heart stopped.

Her first instinct was to run. Instead, she took a deep breath and placed her ear against the door. It was a slab of solid wood, but the voices on the other side were so loud and angry, she could hear them anyway.

A cacophony of words seeped through, although, as usual, she couldn't understand a single one. As she pressed her ear closer, the door moved ever so slightly, making a faint *click* as it pressed against its frame.

Suddenly the arguing inside ceased and rapid footsteps thundered toward the door. Beatrice flung herself around the corner, slipping behind a tapestry that hung on the wall.

The door opened with an angry *clack*. Beatrice held her breath and squeezed her eyes shut.

twenty-seven

INTO THE BELLY OF THE PALACE

"Non ti preoccupare. Era solo il vento!"[1] came a male voice from inside the library.

"Sì, va be',"[2] said another gruffly, mere inches from Beatrice's face.

The door slammed and Beatrice exhaled, reeling at the close call. So much for the secret passageway through the library. So much for her entire plan.

She slipped off her sandals and retraced her steps

. . . .

1.   "Don't worry. It was just the wind!"
2.   "Yeah, ok."

on tiptoe until she deemed it safe to put them back on. She'd just have to find another way down into the ruins under the palace. Easier said than done.

She turned a few more corners and walked into a rectangular room dominated by a large dining table with twenty high-backed chairs. Noticing a peculiarity on the wall, she decided to investigate. Four wooden beams formed a square, a bit like the frame of a window, except there was no window. Just wall.

Suddenly everything she'd been talking and thinking about over the past week became vividly real. She was standing in the selfsame room where Muzio Mattei and his father-in-law had dined that fateful night, over four hundred years ago. It was from this very window—which was a window no longer—that the Turtle Fountain had been seen for the first time.

Thanks to that fountain, a young woman's happiness had been destroyed. It didn't matter that she'd lived four centuries ago. To Beatrice, Caterina had become as real and intimate as if she were her own big sister.

She wrenched her gaze from the walled-up window and saw another curiosity, this time on the opposite wall. She walked over to inspect it.

A tiny wooden door was embedded in the wall. It looked like some sort of built-in cabinet. She tugged it open, unable to resist her curiosity. If it was a cabinet, it was an odd one. There was nothing inside, not even shelves—just an empty hole in the wall, a wooden cube.

As if a voice were telling her she'd missed something in the dark, she impulsively reached inside, feeling along the cabinet's smooth interior. Her hand pressed the bottom and the cabinet quivered with a strident *creak*.

Beatrice jumped back. Warily, she reached into the cabinet again, and this time she pressed harder. Sure enough, the entire box sank a few inches. Could it be a dumbwaiter? She'd read about them in novels set in Victorian times: mini-elevators that brought hot dishes from the kitchen up to the dining room and took the dirty plates back down. They were usually operated by handheld cranks in the kitchens below.

Suddenly she got a crazy idea. Ignoring every rational bone in her (thankfully) petite body, she impulsively climbed into the dark, cramped box, pulling her bag in with her. Under the force of her weight, the dumbwaiter instantly began its rickety descent. She had just enough time to pull the little door closed.

All was blackness. The creaking rang out in the dark, and Beatrice prayed the men in the library couldn't hear it. It seemed like an impossibly long way down. Seated with her legs crossed and her head ducked, her upper back pressed against the top of the box, she tried not to imagine what would happen if the dumbwaiter never reached its destination. Or if the lower door was locked, or blocked in some way.

She hadn't stopped to think about these possibilities before recklessly hopping inside. But in the tiny black space, she couldn't help visualizing what would happen if she got trapped. The slow, agonizing death from suffocation, her father's panic when he returned home to find his only daughter missing, her contorted skeleton found decades later . . .

Her descent slowed and, as if her worst nightmare were coming true, the wooden box came to a lethargic stop. She couldn't catch her breath. Her head, by now nearly resting on her knee, was spinning. Blackness gave way to big orange splotches. Her hands frantically pressed against the walls of the dumbwaiter. She wanted to scream but couldn't find her voice.

Her right hand punched out wildly and the door flew open. She tumbled out of the box and landed with a thud on a cold stone floor.

Cool, welcome air flooded her lungs. She got to her feet and was hit with a head rush. Red spots twirled in front of her eyes like polka dots on a Spanish dancer's dress. She waited for her vision to return, and when it didn't, she concluded that the room she was standing in was as dark as the dumbwaiter.

She must be in the kitchen. Where else would the dumbwaiter lead? She felt in the dark and located her bag where it had fallen on the floor. She unzipped it and fished out her flashlight.

She switched it on and shined it around a large, stark room that looked more like a laboratory than a kitchen. Long wooden worktables filled the space and the floor was tiled with a dull gray stone. There were giant sinks as deep as bathtubs and a fireplace big enough to walk inside. Dozens of hooks hung over the tables, where gleaming copper pots must have once dangled. Nothing but cobwebs hung from them now. Judging from the layers of dust on the tables, the kitchen hadn't been used for decades, maybe centuries. Who knew the last time a human had walked through these rooms? Who knew what she'd find lurking around the corner?

Steeling herself, she grabbed her bag and followed the beam of her flashlight through the kitchen's only doorway and into a narrow corridor. To the right was a small wooden door with a rounded top that barely reached her shoulder. To the left stood a doorframe, walled up like the window upstairs. The kitchen must have been sealed off from the rest of the house years ago.

The tiny wooden door was her only option. It was rough and splintered with an iron latch instead of a handle. She tried to pull it back, but it didn't budge. Pulling harder, she managed to move it about a millimeter. She'd need both hands. She stood her flashlight on the ground and the upward beam turned her shadow into a grotesque monster.

Using the force of her entire body, she managed to pull back the latch, but even unfastened, the door remained tightly sealed, its boards swollen with time. After a few minutes of futile pushing and pulling, Beatrice gave it an exasperated kick. The warped wood splintered at the sides as the door swung open.

She snatched her flashlight and shined it into the

void. Ducking under the low doorframe, she almost lost her balance and stumbled down a flight of rough stone steps that led to a cavern below. Her arms bristled as the temperature dropped with every step.

Her flashlight illuminated a narrow space with a dirt floor, a barrel-vaulted ceiling, and crumbling brick walls that looked a thousand years old. Along the wall squatted fat wooden wine barrels, covered with cobwebs and filth. She wrinkled her nose at the stench of centuries of decay. She scanned the cellar for a door or passageway. Nothing.

Another dead end? Panic seeped through her body, as hot and unstoppable as lava. As she took a deep breath to slow her furious heart, Caterina's eyes flashed into her brain. *Only you can do this.*

She braced herself and ventured deeper into the cellar. On the far wall sat more wine barrels. One stood apart from the others, positioned upright instead of on its side and flush against the wall, as if it were hiding something.

Beatrice edged up to the barrel and shined her flashlight around the back to reveal a chink in the wall. The barrel was empty and the wood was rotten, so one good shove was enough to move it aside, exposing the opening of a long, narrow tunnel that stretched into the distance. She shined her light inside, but the tunnel reached well beyond its beam. Crawling through a dark, dusty tunnel with no idea where it led—or even *if* it led anywhere—was not an especially appealing idea. Not that she had any other options.

She knew she was just postponing the inevitable, but she decided to consult Caterina's map. It showed the path from the library, *not* from the kitchens of course, but she figured it was worth a look. As she spread the map out on the gravelly ground, her flashlight flickered and went out. She was plunged into blackness.

Gripped with panic, she shook the flashlight violently. The light mercifully came back on, but how much time until the battery died completely? Stuffing that worrisome question into the back of her mind, she stared at the map, trying to make sense of its perplexing squiggles.

It was at that precise moment that Beatrice Archer had one of the most brilliant ideas of her life to date. She dug out the photocopy of the Isola Mattei floor plan and quickly located her position. Then she placed Caterina's map of the ruins directly on top. When she shined the flashlight on the aged parchment, it became translucent, the lines on the floor plan showing through, plain as day. She lined up the markings of the cavea with the curving walls of the floor plan beneath and pinpointed where she was on Caterina's map.

Nothing on the map looked like a tunnel, but if her calculations were correct, she wasn't far from the curving wall of the theater—and the telltale X just beyond. At the very least, she'd be heading in the right direction. She folded up the papers and tucked them into the pocket of her dress. Ignoring her hammering heart, she ducked into the tunnel.

Cobwebs and dirt rained down on her head and the thought of the hideous pests that might be lurking nearby made her shudder. The tunnel seemed to go on forever. After hitting her head more than once, she decided it would be easier to crawl. Fumbling with the flashlight, she squirmed her way through the dirt and dust, gravel cutting into her bare knees. Was it just her imagination, or was the tunnel getting tighter? Was it beginning to slope downward?

She fought the urge to panic as the walls closed in around her.

Just when she'd convinced herself she'd never get

out alive, the tunnel abruptly ended. With a final scramble, she was out. She gulped down several breaths and dusted herself off, then shined the flashlight in front of her.

Nothing could have prepared her for the sight of the ancient theater rising before her. Her meager beam couldn't illuminate the entire structure at once, but as she flashed it here and there, the theater slowly materialized before her eyes, as if it were waking from a centuries-long sleep.

Rising from a pavement of broad, dusty flagstones, the curving outer wall was a series of massive arches. A shorter set of arches stood upon the first, their tops disappearing into the ceiling. The upper levels were long gone.

Beatrice shivered, and not because of the cold. She'd succeeded in finding the ancient ruins, but she was unspeakably alone. And what was worse, no one alive knew where she was.

twenty-eight

DISCOVERY IN THE DARK

Despite the palpable stillness of the underground lair, the past rumbled into life around her. Beatrice scuffed her sandal on an ancient flagstone, thinking of all those who had trod that same spot, imagining what they would have seen: a towering marble-faced theater bustling with loud-voiced merchants, scruffy beggar children, senators in togas. She pictured soldiers shouting orders from prancing horses and wealthy matrons being carried in litters by long-suffering slaves. It was thousands of years away, and yet, it had happened *right here.* The thought both fascinated and terrified her, and with an unexpected pang, she found herself wishing Marco were there to experience it with her.

On shaking limbs, Beatrice approached the theater. She placed a sweaty palm on a gritty stone archway and the weight of the centuries rippled through her. She stepped inside and a wide curving corridor stretched to her left and right. Beyond it stood an inner wall of identical arches. She peered through one to find a vast wedge-shaped space with a barrel-vaulted ceiling. Just like in the tunnel, the feeble beam of her flashlight did little to illuminate the gloom beyond. But if the map was correct, one of these spaces held—at least at one time in history—Caterina's secret room. Would the turtles be there, as her intuition assured her, or was she on a wild-goose chase?

Only one way to find out.

She forced herself to walk slowly and deliberately, shining her light into each wedge-shaped chamber and counting them in turn. After passing eight empty spaces, she began to lose hope. But as she aimed the flashlight into the ninth chamber, instead of being eaten up by impenetrable blackness, the beam reflected off a shiny surface five or six feet in front of her. Her breath caught in her throat.

With halting steps, she inched toward the unknown

surface and came face-to-face with a broad antique wooden door, conspicuously out of place in the abandoned archaeological site. It had no handle, just a big brass knocker in the middle. She pushed tentatively, half expecting it to be locked. Instead, the door swung open with a satisfying groan. Beatrice was standing on the threshold of the secret room.

She swept the flashlight around, taking in a space so contrary to its setting that it seemed unreal. Intricate tapestries and unlit torches hung on the walls, oriental carpets covered the rough ground, and an ornate writing desk and chair stood against one wall. A lavish divan and a leather trunk sat at the far end of the room where the walls narrowed and the ceiling inclined sharply, almost all the way to the ground. A thrill zipped up her spine as she realized she was standing directly under the rising seats of the ancient theater.

Through her mind danced images of Roman slaves laying the walls brick by brick and theatergoers climbing to their seats to watch a performance. Most vividly of all, she saw Caterina, the woman whose face was now burned onto her brain, sitting at this very desk, putting words to her lonely thoughts. She was so overwhelmed by these visions that she almost forgot about the turtles. Almost.

She ventured deeper inside. A cursory inspection revealed no bronze turtles and for a split second her old doubts came rushing back. Maybe she'd gotten it all wrong, like Marco had said.

The flashlight beam wavered. With a thunderclap to the gut, Beatrice realized she didn't have a moment to lose and sprang into action. The desk? No, the fussy drawers were too small to hold the turtles. Her eyes flicked around the room, searching for possible hiding places.

She crept deeper into the chamber and her head brushed the slanted ceiling, sending down a cascade of cobwebs. As she shook the debris of ages from her hair, her flashlight flickered off and darkness enveloped her. This time, no amount of shaking would make it work again. She threw the useless object to the ground.

In the sudden and total darkness, Beatrice's heart thumped in her ears. Visions of spiders and rats swam before her unseeing eyes. She stamped them out, picturing instead the room she'd seen just moments before. She stumbled forward, arms outstretched, ducking to avoid the low ceiling. After a few more steps, she tripped over an unwieldy object and landed on it with a *smack*. She ran her hands across its smooth hard surfaces. The trunk!

She knelt beside it, and after fumbling with the latch, she eased it open. The hinges creaked like the cry of a bat. She reached inside blindly but her hands recoiled instinctively, as if they feared to meet with the withered bones of an ancient skeleton, maybe even the skeleton of Caterina herself. Her stomach lurched at the thought but she forced her unwilling hands into the trunk.

They touched neither bones nor metal, but soft, feltlike fabric: the last thing she expected. Still, there was something hard underneath. Grabbing fistfuls of fabric, she pulled a bulky weight out of the trunk and onto her lap, her heart hammering. She tore at the fabric until she touched cool metal.

Beatrice's eager fingers explored the object's every curve and sinew, noting a rounded shell, four protruding feet, a curling tail, and an unmistakable head. She was holding one of Bernini's turtles.

She cradled her prize as if it were a lost child, wishing she could admire it with her eyes and not just her hands. Euphoria bubbled up inside her, but she didn't have time to savor the moment. She had work to do. She pulled the turtles out of the trunk one by one, handling them clumsily in the dark. They'd looked so delicate sitting atop the fountain, but in reality they were the size of small watermelons and nearly as heavy. She arranged two in her canvas bag and two in her backpack. Meanwhile the seconds ticked relentlessly by.

She heaved on the backpack and hoisted the strained canvas bag onto one shoulder, staggering out of the room under the nearly impossible weight. As she turned into the theater's inner corridor, she heard the rumble of voices echoing off the ancient stones. The men were coming for the turtles. It was only a matter of minutes, perhaps seconds, before they discovered they were gone. She had to hide them, fast. Only then could she concentrate on saving herself.

With nowhere else to go, Beatrice turned her inner compass back toward the tunnel. But would she find it in the dark? She couldn't run blindly, and besides, her burden wouldn't allow it. Instead she slowly and deliberately retraced her steps along the curving corridor until she felt her way through the archway and out of the theater. She inched forward, her free hand outstretched, tripping over stones and bits of ancient debris. At last her fingertips brushed a wall as rough as sandpaper.

Flashlight beams bounced off the nearby walls, making Beatrice's mouth go dry. They were getting closer. Blinking back tears as the straps of the bag cut into her shoulder, she shuffled from side to side, kicking at the wall. Finally she kicked into emptiness—the tunnel.

Her stomach contracted at the thought of crawling back through the impossibly tight space, but the footsteps beating ever louder told her she had no choice.

She eased the cloth bag off her shoulder and shrugged off her backpack, placing them both into the mouth of the tunnel. She thrust the bags—and their precious cargo—in as far as her arms would reach, then scrambled into the tunnel behind them. Pushing the cumbersome turtles while crawling through the narrow pitch-black tunnel was no easy feat. A sloth would have moved faster.

She hadn't gone more than a few feet when angry voices rang out behind her. The tunnel was suddenly flooded with light and a rough hand clamped around her ankle. Instinctively, her arms flailed out, trying to grab hold of something—anything. But it did her no good. With a vicious yank she was hauled out of the tunnel feet first. A pair of burly arms wrapped around her like an angry snake and a meaty paw clapped over her mouth.

Beatrice tried to scream, but it came out a whimper as someone lifted her off her feet. She thrashed and squirmed, but the grip didn't loosen.

The beam of a wildly jostling flashlight provided fleeting glimpses of her surroundings: rough stone walls, a hairy wrist, feet shuffling along a dirt floor. She recoiled in horror at the realization that they were carrying her deeper and deeper into the ruins.

Suddenly the second man grabbed her legs and her two tormentors began dragging her up a steep flight of stairs. She kicked out her legs, twisting and flailing to try to throw them off-balance. She was rewarded for her efforts by a sharp pain on the top of her head, a tingling in her ears, and then nothing.

twenty-nine

INTERROGATION AND
REVELATION

Gibberish. Melodic gibberish, but gibberish nonetheless. At least that's what it sounded like.

Beatrice lifted her lids and was greeted by a hammering headache and clouds before her eyes. As her vision cleared, she took in the strangely familiar surroundings: a mahogany desk, leather sofas, towering bookshelves, all bathed in low light. She was back in the palace library, lying on a couch.

A quick glance at her person revealed she was a mess. Her bare knees were caked in dirt, her feet and sandals were black with grime, and her polka-dot dress was unrecognizable. She didn't even want to imagine what her hair looked like.

Across the room, two men in dark suits were arguing in Italian with a third person, hidden from view.

"Ascolta un attimo."[1] The bright, round tones of a feminine voice floated across the room.

Beatrice's ears perked up. She lifted her throbbing head to get a better look and her eyes bulged.

"Ah, guarda chi si è svegliata!"[2]

One of the men stomped across the room. He had short black hair that was thinning on top and sharp features. It was Mr. Beak Nose, the man she'd seen in this very library just days before.

"DOVE SONO?"[3] he bellowed, inches from her nose.

Beatrice recoiled. No one had ever screamed in her face like that. She lay speechless, trying to remember why she'd gotten herself into this mess.

"Dove sono, bambina impudente?"[4] His angular face was twisted by rage.

. . . .

1. "Listen a moment."
2. "Ah, look who's awake!"
3. "WHERE ARE THEY?"
4. "Where are they, impudent child?"

"*Non parla italiano*," said the woman indifferently.

Beatrice felt the urge to shout that she did *too* speak Italian—at least a little bit—but on second thought, perhaps it wasn't the most opportune moment to bring that up.

The man took hold of her shoulders and yanked her up to a seating position. He took a deep breath, as if it were taking all his self-control not to tear her to bits.

"Where are they?" he growled.

"Who?" was all Beatrice could manage.

"*Le tartarughe*, you little brat! Where have you hidden those blasted turtles?" He sprayed her face with saliva.

Beatrice winced. "I don't know what you're talking about."

"You know exactly what I'm talking about." His dark eyes bored into hers like a pair of daggers. "I don't know how you did it, but you found the turtles and now you've hidden them. We've searched, but it's a maze down there." For a moment, in his wild eyes, Beatrice glimpsed a desperate man, but he turned back into a bully in no time. "If you don't start talking this second, you'll regret the day you were born."

Beatrice shuddered in spite of herself.

"TELL ME WHERE YOU PUT THEM!" he screamed, shaking her like a rag doll.

"*Vincenzo, basta! La stai terrorizzando!*"[5] The woman's and the girl's eyes met. Beatrice felt sick with betrayal as she stared silently at her Italian teacher. A dozen questions flooded her mind, but she couldn't form words to a single one.

"*Bene!*"[6] bellowed the man called Vincenzo. "She *should* be terrified! That's what she deserves for meddling in other people's affairs." He glanced nervously at his wristwatch. To Beatrice he added snidely, "Stick to your dollies, little girl. This is a matter for adults."

Beatrice burned with indignation. "I have no idea where these turtles are or why they're so important," she lied. "But even if I did, I wouldn't tell *you*!" she snapped, shocked at her own audacity.

"Oh, really?" Vincenzo crooned sarcastically. "Then how do you explain this?" He popped open a slick laptop computer. The screen flickered to life and Beatrice could see herself in grainy black and white. She was in the secret room, fumbling with a flashlight

· ·

5. "Vincenzo, enough! You're terrorizing her!"
6. "Good!"

and shaking cobwebs from her hair. The flashlight went out but Beatrice's movements were still visible. Night-vision surveillance cameras!

Vincenzo slammed the computer shut and crossed back to where she sat. He checked his watch again, although less than a minute had passed. Beatrice inched away from him, rubbing her shoulders where he'd grasped her.

"Now, leettle girl," he said through clenched teeth, "you will tell me what you did with those turtles, or I will throw you back down into the ruins, where you will die of suffocation and starvation. I guarantee no one will ever find you."

The hairs on the back of Beatrice's neck stood on end. With a lump in her throat, she decided to throw caution to the wind; she hadn't gotten this far by playing it safe.

"Even if I told you, you'd probably throw me down there anyway, so I don't really have anything to lose, do I?"

Vincenzo issued a guttural growl. "*Ugo!*" he barked. "*Vieni qui.*"[7]

. . . .

7. "Come here."

The beefy thing she'd seen on her first visit to the palace plodded across the room. Ugo was an ogre with massive arms and a half circle of black hair around the back of his head. He stood at Vincenzo's side and stared Beatrice down. Two beady black eyes glittered under a solitary eyebrow that wriggled across his forehead like a big, fat caterpillar.

"Now, leettle girl," Vincenzo continued, "before I lose my temper—"

"Too late," quipped Beatrice.

"Do not interrupt me, you intolerable girl! This is not a game," said Vincenzo, raising his hand as if to slap her.

Beatrice stared up at him, refusing to cower.

Instead, Vincenzo ran a finger under his collar and checked his watch for the umpteenth time, sweat glistening on his forehead. "You will tell me where you hid those turtles," he said desperately, "or my associate Ugo here will help you remember." Ugo smirked.

Beatrice gulped nervously but decided to call their bluff. "You can do what you like with me," she said defiantly, her eyes darkening, "but I'll never let you sell those turtles to some French billionaire!"

Vincenzo's mouth dropped open. "How did

you . . ." He stopped midsentence and spun around on Ginevra. "What have you told this child?"

"Nothing!" Ginevra garbled, bafflement scribbled across her forehead. "I have told her *nothing*. I cannot imagine how she knows thees!"

"That explains how she got inside. I should have known you would turn on me and try to steal the turtles for yourself. But to recruit the assistance of a *child*!"

"Thees is preposterous! She has nothing to do with thees. . . ." Her voice rose an octave as she switched to Italian.

And that's when Beatrice got her second brilliant idea of the night.

"Ginevra, why don't you tell them the truth?" Beatrice shouted. Vincenzo's head swiveled around. "Tell them how you planned to steal the turtles for yourself! That's right," she said to Vincenzo's gaping face, "if you want to find them so badly, ask *her*. She told me where to hide them!"

"She ees lying!" Ginevra protested.

"Think about it," Beatrice continued. "She's my Italian teacher; I live just across the square. Don't you think it's a bit too much of a coincidence?"

"She ees making thees all up!" Ginevra's voice was high-pitched and desperate.

"Come on! How else would I have known *exactly* where the turtles were hidden?"

Vincenzo's eyes were black as murder. As he opened his mouth to emit what was sure to be a nasty stream of abuse, a metallic ring pealed out. He took another frantic look at his watch, then whipped out a squealing cell phone.

Before answering, he addressed Ugo. "*Controlla la bambina!*"[8] he commanded. Then, turning a pair of grim eyes on Ginevra, he added, "*Controlla tutte e due. Non perderle di vista!*"[9] He strode out of the library and slammed the door.

Ugo crossed his arms over his chest with a sneer, clearly relishing his job as watchdog. Luckily, he didn't seem to understand English.

Ginevra turned on Beatrice, her usually laughing eyes as cold as ice. "How dare you lie about me like that?"

"How dare *you* conspire with these thugs to steal art?" Beatrice continued.

. . . .

8. "Watch the child!"
9. "Watch both of them. Don't let them out of your sight!"

260

"You wouldn't understand." Ginevra turned away haughtily. "Besides," she huffed, "I don't have to explain myself to a *child*!"

A child. So that was how she saw her. Someone whose opinion didn't matter, who could be lied to and dismissed. Rage and indignation began to build up inside of her, until she could hold them in no longer.

"Maybe you don't have to explain yourself to *me*, but you'll have to explain yourself to the police! As soon as I get out of here, I'm going straight to the cops to tell them you're an art thief masquerading as an art history student."

"Eet's not like that. You don't know the whole story."

"There's no possible excuse for stealing art."

"What do you know about eet, you naive leettle reech girl!"

"Rich girl?" said Beatrice, aghast. "We're not rich."

"Oh, no?" Ginevra scoffed. "You leeve in a penthouse in Piazza Mattei. You are reech enough, *cara mia*."

"Even if I were, what does that have to do with anything?"

Ginevra looked at Beatrice for a long moment.

Then, with a sigh, she sunk into a leather armchair. She drew her arms around herself, shivering slightly despite the sweltering night.

"My father was an art dealer, so were his father and his grandfather, back five generations. My father was training me to take over one day; I was to be the first woman to run the family business." Her voice rang with pride. "I studied art history. My dream was to turn our leettle business into an important gallery and auction house.

"Six months ago, my father told me he had secured an important client. A member of an old noble Roman family needed to sell hees entire art collection, queeckly. Massive gambling debts. We were to organize an auction of the works. But before the contract was signed, my father had a heart attack. He died instantly.

"My world was turned upside down. Just like his client, my father had also been secretly in debt. His body wasn't cold before his creditors came calling. Unfortunately, *we* do not have a palace and a private art collection to save us," she said with a dry little laugh. "I went to appraise the Mattei collection in my father's place, hoping that if I could just keep that one client, we might be able to hold on to the business. But although Vincenzo's collection was vast, eet was not valuable enough to cover all of his debts." She paused, her look of anguish suddenly replaced with a gleam of mischief. "The turtles on the fountain right outside, however, *were*."

"But those turtles don't belong to the Mattei family!" Beatrice burst out. "They belong to the city of Rome!"

"An eensignificant detail." Conceit shone in Ginevra's eyes at the brilliant plan she had hatched. "Suddenly I saw a way out. Together, Vincenzo and I devised a plan to steal the turtles. I planned the particulars and found an unscrupulous buyer through my father's contacts, as well as an artist to re-create believable replicas. Vincenzo took care of the negotiations and hired a thief to do the dirty work. We planned to split the money fifty-fifty. Vincenzo would get to keep hees palace and art collection, and my family would be saved."

Beatrice felt a mixture of anger, betrayal, and sympathy for the woman who'd been her first Italian teacher, and—she had thought—her friend. She was the first person to pronounce her name in the deliciously Italian way, the first to help her understand this crazy, beautiful language. But none of that made up for the fact that she was a thief, and an unrepentant one at that.

Beatrice gritted her teeth. "If you think you can make me feel sorry for you, you're dreaming. I'm not going to let you get away with this."

Ginevra's eyes hardened into puddles of black ice. "I am sorry to hear that. If that ees truly the case, I am afraid you are unlikelee to leave thees palace alive."

thirty

DÉJÀ VU WITH A TWIST

Beatrice and Ginevra were glaring at each other unblinking when the library door flung open and Vincenzo marched back in.

"Still scheming, I see?"

Ginevra leaped to her feet. "Tell heem you were lying!"

Beatrice's gaze slid from Ginevra's furious eyes to Vincenzo's menacing ones. She took a deep breath. "Everything I said was true."

Ginevra shot her a look of pure hate and the temperature in the room seemed to drop by twenty degrees. Vincenzo and Ginevra began a shouting match in Italian, with Ugo interjecting every so often. With her captors' attention distracted, Beatrice took the opportunity to plan her escape.

Unfortunately, the three coconspirators were blocking the doorway. Perhaps a window? Moving as little as possible, Beatrice peeked over her shoulder to see if she could fit out of one of them.

Through the gauzy curtains she could make out the piazza. Glancing back at Ginevra and the two men, still in heated debate, she decided to make a run for it. She slipped off the couch and hurried to the window. Just as she ducked behind the curtain, she stopped short. She stared down into the piazza, unable to believe her eyes.

Clang!

She felt like she was reliving a nightmare, or having some kind of freaky déjà vu.

Clang!

Once again, the same lanky thief was standing on the lip of the fountain, using a crowbar to remove one of the turtles. But this time he wasn't alone.

A second figure crouched in the shadows on the opposite side of the fountain: watching, waiting, by the look of it ready to pounce. Beatrice couldn't make out his face, but the messy head of curls was unmistakable.

Marco! Her stomach did a somersault. What was he doing risking his neck for a bunch of fakes? Except Marco never believed they were fakes. She reached for the window latch, but it was useless—it was far too high to jump.

It all happened in the space of an instant. Marco sprang from his hiding place. As nimble as a tightrope walker, he hopped over the fountain railing and yanked the thief's leg, sending him tumbling from his perch. The thief landed in the fountain and the turtle he had just detached flew out of his grasp. Marco dived for the delicate bronze sculpture but he was too late: it collided with the cobblestones with an almighty crash.

The thief righted himself and lunged at Marco. Beatrice clamped her hand over her mouth to keep from screaming. She didn't notice the arguing behind her cease or the heavy footsteps as Vincenzo approached.

"Trying to escape, you leettle red devil?" He seized her. Then he noticed the scene outside and stopped in his tracks. *"Oh, cavolo!"*[1] He pushed Beatrice aside and flew out of the room.

Ginevra and Ugo ran to the window in time to see Marco and the thief taking swipes at each other. *"Oddio!"*[2] exclaimed Ginevra. "Who ees *that*? Another blasted American brat?"

"He's as Roman as you are and he doesn't want you and your thug partner destroying that fountain any more than I do!"

"Why cannot you mind your own beezness?"

Beatrice didn't bother answering. She had to help Marco.

She watched from the window as Vincenzo strode into the piazza below. He made straight for Marco, who was scrambling to gather the other turtles. Catching him off guard, Vincenzo grabbed his arm, spun him around, and punched him square in the jaw. Marco toppled over and the turtles came crashing down with him. Beatrice didn't wait to see what would happen next.

"Where do you think you're going?" Ginevra

. . . .

1. "Oh, drat!"
2. "Oh, God!"

shouted as Beatrice raced to the door that was now unguarded. Ugo, distracted by the commotion outside, was too slow to catch her as she sprinted out of the library.

She flew down the portrait gallery with Ugo the ogre in hot pursuit. She rounded the corner into the grand hall and sped down the stairs to where the door to the courtyard had been left wide open. At the bottom of the steps she slammed into Vincenzo, who was carrying a writhing Marco over his shoulder. They tumbled over backward.

As Marco scrambled to his feet, Ugo pounced, snatching him up as if he were no bigger than a puppet. Meanwhile Vincenzo grabbed Beatrice's arms and wrenched them behind her back. "Let go of me, you evil art thief!"

Marco did a double take. "What are you doing here?"

"What are *you* doing here?" she demanded back.

But their captors gave them no time to catch up. Instead they dragged them into the library, where Ginevra was waiting with a rope, a sneer of triumph twitching on her lips. Ugo placed Marco back on his feet but kept his meaty arms wrapped around him tight.

Despite being squeezed like a tube of toothpaste, Marco was grinning ear to ear. He looked Beatrice up and down. "You're a mess!" he said with a wry smile. "What exactly have you been up to?"

"Don't ask," Beatrice groaned. "You don't look so hot yourself." Marco's lip was bleeding and his jaw was already turning purple from Vincenzo's punch.

"*Legali!*"[3] Vincenzo ordered.

Ugo pinned them back-to-back with hands the size of baseball mitts while Ginevra tied them together. As Beatrice fumed at the rough treatment, Marco found her hand and squeezed it. A knot of guilt took form in the pit of her stomach and soon she was up to her neck in regret. Why had she jumped to conclusions, just because he hadn't agreed with her? Her instincts may have been spot-on about *things*, but they were useless when it came to people.

Once their bonds were so tight they could barely move, Vincenzo marched ominously toward them. Beatrice winced inwardly but put on a brave face. She refused to let him know he scared her.

"Why didn't you tell me what you were planning?"

. . . .

3. "Tie them up!"

Marco whispered. "We could have worked together!"

"I tried, but you wouldn't listen!" she hissed back.

"Silence!" commanded Vincenzo. "You will speak when I tell you, and not before. Now, young man, I don't know how you're involved in this, but I'll deal with you later. First, *Signorina Beatrice*," he mocked, "you will tell me what you know and how you know it."

"I told you, from Ginevra."

"Stop lying!" he barked, but she could tell he wasn't convinced. "You tell me the truth right now, leettle girl." He wagged a finger in front of her nose. "How did you get into the ruins, and where have you hidden those turtles? Cooperate, and we *may* let you live. Stay silent and you and your friend will suffer a fate worse than death." He jerked his head toward Ugo, who rolled up his shirtsleeves with a beastly smile. He cracked his hairy knuckles and advanced with slow heavy steps until he was towering over them. Time and Beatrice's brilliant ideas were running out.

Marco was being awfully quiet, she thought resentfully. He was making slight, repetitive movements, probably attempting to cut their ropes somehow, Beatrice assumed. Not a bad idea, but even unbound, how would they escape with Ugo the guard dog pant-ing over them?

"So, what's it going to be?" Vincenzo snapped. "Are you going to be a good leettle girl and tell me what I want to know, or—"

His pocket rang furiously, causing him to leave his threat unfinished. He dug out his phone and frowned. *"Sì?"*

A voice shouted indistinct words from the other end of the line and the color drained from Vincenzo's face. He turned away, whispering frantically into the phone.

Beatrice squirmed, trying in vain to slip her hands out of the ropes. Ugo chuckled at her futile efforts. He was so close she could smell his rotten breath.

Vincenzo thrust his phone back into his pocket, his face pasty and strained. *"Controllali bene,"*[4] he said to Ugo sharply. *"Torno subito."*[5] He walked out of the library as if he were on the way to his own execution.

Less than a minute later, several sets of footsteps beat down the hallway. Vincenzo walked in first,

. . . .

4. "Watch them closely."
5. "I'll be right back."

wearing a look of pure panic. Behind him marched Monsieur Cambriolage, impeccably dressed as always, flanked by two bearlike thugs who made Ugo look like a runt by comparison.

One of the thugs had Luca, the scrawny thief, by the scruff of his neck. He looked even more dejected than Vincenzo. The other one was carrying four bronze turtles as if they were no heavier than plastic toys.

"What is ze meaning of zis?" roared Cambriolage, taking one of the turtles from thug number two. The turtle was covered in scratches and its head was smashed in. "Zese are damaged goods! I paid you a fortune for zese sculptures and you deliver zem in zis condition?"

He grabbed a second turtle with its foot bent backward and deep gashes across the shell. "I demand ze money back, immediately!"

He glanced at Beatrice and Marco, bound together on the couch. "Don't tell me you traffic in children as well!" His lip curled in disgust. Then he took a second look at Beatrice. "You!" he spat, a spark of recognition now glinting in his eyes. "First I meet you at ze auction viewing in zis very palace, zen I see you in ze embassy wiz Mademoiselle Ginevra, and now 'ere? Who are you, and 'ow are you mixed up in all of zis?"

"At the embassy? With Ginevra? So you *are* in this together!" Vincenzo spat at Ginevra. She opened her mouth to protest, but he grabbed her wrist and silenced her with a murderous look. "*Ci penso a te dopo,*"[6] he hissed in her ear.

He turned back to Cambriolage. "Monsieur, these impudent children are the cause of the damage of the turtles. But believe me, they will soon regret it."

Beatrice couldn't believe Vincenzo was blaming *them*. As if *they* were the criminals!

"He's lying!" she shouted. "And those aren't Bernini's turtles! They're fakes, just like you suspected! He's been fooling you all along!"

Vincenzo's mouth hung open as his night went from bad to worse.

"*Sacré bleu!*" Cambriolage stared down at the turtle in his hands. "But how on earth do you know zis? Explain yourself, girl!"

"Untie us and I'll tell you everything."

Cambriolage shouted to one of his men, who

. . . .

6. "I'll deal with you later."

flicked out a knife and sliced them free. So much for Marco's valiant effort, Beatrice thought, rubbing her rope-burned wrists.

"You're going to take the word of a delinquent foreign child? Over a member of the Italian aristocracy?" sputtered Vincenzo.

"Aristocracy? Pshaw! Money talks, my friend, not titles! Ah, *mon Dieu*," he lamented, "this is what I get for working with amateurs!" He turned to Beatrice, "You were saying, *ma'moiselle*?"

Everyone turned to Beatrice. Vincenzo's face was a mask of dread.

Just as she opened her mouth to speak, not sure whether to tell the truth or a lie, a police siren wailed from the piazza outside. Everyone froze. Vincenzo's look of dread turned to terror and Monsieur Cambriolage no longer looked quite so confident himself.

The siren stopped and a voice boomed over a loud speaker, shouting orders from the square. Everyone exchanged horror-filled looks and after one tense moment, panic erupted. Ginevra yanked her arm free from Vincenzo's grasp. Vincenzo barked at Ugo. One of the French thugs looked for a place to hide the damaged turtles while Cambriolage screamed at

Vincenzo, demanding his client's money back. Luca the scrawny thief searched for a way to escape, but the other henchman refused to let go of his collar.

In all the confusion, no one noticed the quiet Italian boy sneak out to let the police in. Beatrice wasn't far behind, and they got to the front door just as the police began to kick it in.

thirty-one

THE FOUR PROTECTORS

It had been a busy night for the local police station. First they'd gotten an emergency call that a thirteen-year-old girl had gone missing in the vicinity of Piazza Mattei. As they prepared to investigate, they received another call but could hear only muffled voices. *Threatening* muffled voices.

When Beatrice thought Marco was trying to cut their ropes, he'd actually been using his cell phone behind his back, calling the police and recording the incriminating conversation. Once the police had traced the call to the Mattei Palace, a squad car was dispatched within minutes. When the officers arrived in the piazza to find the turtles missing from the fountain, they knew they were in for a long night.

Meanwhile, across town, Mr. Archer got a worrying call of his own. After reluctantly leaving his daughter at the concert, he'd asked Signora Costaguti to keep her eye out and make sure she got home safely. But midnight came and went with no sign of Beatrice. Mirella alerted him, and he called the police and rushed home. But the sharp old *signora* had her own ideas about where Beatrice might be. When the police eventually called to tell Mr. Archer his daughter had been identified inside the Mattei Palace, Mirella wasn't surprised in the least, and she insisted on accompanying him to the palace across the square.

When Augustus Archer stepped into the library, his usually smiling face was haggard with worry. Beatrice barreled straight for him and pitched herself into his arms. She hadn't realized until that moment how close she'd come to never seeing him again. She squeezed until she felt like her arms would fall off, and he squeezed back just as hard.

Once they'd released each other from their epic hug, Mr. Archer's gaze swept the room. As he took in the half-dozen people in handcuffs, the damaged sculptures, the police officers, and the boy with a bloody lip, the relieved smile slid from his face. "Beatrice Archer, what the devil is going on?"

Since the police wanted to hear the exact same information, Marco translated as Beatrice haltingly told her story. She described how she'd witnessed the turtles being stolen Monday night, and how no one had believed her. Here she shot her dad a pointed look. "But just minutes after they were ripped off the fountain, the turtles reappeared—like magic! I wouldn't have believed it myself if I hadn't gone down to the piazza to search for clues."

"You did *what*?" her father shouted.

She tried to look remorseful but couldn't quite manage it. "If I hadn't done what I did, the turtles would've been lost forever!" In a tumble of words, it all came out. Beatrice described her first visit to the palace, and the conversation she'd overheard between Vincenzo and Monsieur Cambriolage right in this library, and how she'd concluded that the turtles on the fountain had been replaced with fakes.

"Vincenzo had gambled away his entire fortune and was up to his eyebrows in debt," Beatrice explained. "Instead of selling off his possessions to cover his losses, he decided to hock a set of priceless sculptures that didn't even belong to him."

"*Era tutta l'idea sua!*"[1] shouted Vincenzo, jumping to his feet and aiming an accusing finger at Ginevra. He spewed a barrage of Italian words. One of the officers scribbled furiously in a notebook while another fingered the damaged turtles. They looked thoroughly baffled by the bizarre case.

"But these aren't the real turtles!" Beatrice blurted, sensing they'd failed to grasp the crucial point.

This pronouncement triggered a burst of confusion from the police and grumbling from the French contingent. "*Je le savais.*[2] You lying swindler!" Cambriolage muttered to Vincenzo, as if he weren't in enough trouble himself.

Ginevra seemed only too willing to pay her ex-partner back for his betrayal with a disclosure of her own. "Vincenzo planned to sell Cambriolage the fake turtles and keep the originals for heemself," she announced. "He wanted—what is the Eenglish expression?—to eat hees cake and to have it too."

. . . .

1. "It was all her idea!"
2. "I knew it."

As Vincenzo shot Ginevra a look of pure venom, Beatrice was flooded with vindication. The last piece of the puzzle snapped sublimely into place and she couldn't help throwing Marco a satisfied little smirk.

"But he didn't do it *just* to fatten his art collection."

Every head in the room swiveled around to the unexpected source of this revelation. Old Signora Costaguti had lived in Piazza Mattei longer than any other person alive. She knew all the history of the neighborhood, and most of its secrets. Like the Matteis, the Costagutis were an old Roman family that had been around for centuries. Stories, scandals, and legends were passed down through the generations. Mirella had heard them all.

She began to explain, in her raspy but commanding voice, how the Matteis had been cursed back in the sixteenth century. "No one knows exactly who cursed them," she said. Beatrice and Marco exchanged a meaningful look. "But it is believed to have happened during the time of Muzio Mattei, the ruthless duke who first controlled the gates of the Ghetto, the one who commissioned the fountain.

"After the peak of Mattei power in the seventeenth century," Mirella continued, "the curse began to be fulfilled, and the family started losing not only their wealth, but their social standing as well. A later duke, living about a century after Muzio, commissioned Gian Lorenzo Bernini to create four bronze turtles to adorn the fountain, but they weren't just for decoration. Turtles, in many cultures, symbolize protection and shelter. They were added to ward off the curse, you see, to protect the four branches of the Mattei family, and their four neighboring palaces."

Beatrice's jaw dropped; the connection between past and present was deeper than she could have imagined. "But it didn't do any good!" she couldn't help but interject. "Vincenzo is the only surviving descendant of the family, and three of the four palaces were sold ages ago."

"You are correct." Mirella smiled. "The ultimate fulfillment of the curse is being ushered in during his own lifetime. The last remaining descendant is bankrupt and childless. Once he is gone and the last palace sold, the family will be extinct."

Vincenzo sat glowering, looking less than pleased to be the topic of conversation.

"So," Beatrice reasoned, the entire picture coming into focus at last, "even though he was desperate for cash, he was too superstitious to let the turtles out of family hands. So he decided to have them stolen . . . *twice*. First the real ones, which he hid away in the ruins under the palace and replaced before anyone would notice they'd been taken. And then the *fake* ones, to a rich foreign buyer who'd never know the difference. That way, Vincenzo could pay all his debts, *and* keep the palace and its contents . . . including Bernini's turtles!"

If the police hadn't been satisfied with Beatrice's story, they had Marco's cell phone recording to back it up. The threatening voices of Vincenzo and Cambriolage screeched out of the phone and it was promptly confiscated as evidence.

"You might want to take a look at Monsieur Cambriolage's phone too," Beatrice suggested knowingly. "I think you'll find some *very* interesting information on it."

"The child is making zings up!" scoffed the Frenchman, but his face had gone white.

"I picked his phone up by accident at the French embassy," Beatrice explained, slightly bending the truth. "I took it back right away, of course," she added with a look that was at once innocent and mischievous, "although I couldn't *help* but notice a recent text message with a list of works of art, many of which have gone missing lately. Somehow I don't think it's just a coincidence."

After Marco translated this last bit, an officer searched Cambriolage's pockets, quickly confiscating the phone in question. The vicious look the Frenchman turned on Beatrice was a far cry from his jovial manner of a week before. Never in her life had so many different people looked like they wanted to throttle her. It made her stomach turn.

So she was relieved when the police began rounding up the suspects and leading them out to the waiting squad cars. Vincenzo threw her one last poisonous look as he was shoved out the door. Ugo put his head down and went quietly, like someone familiar with being in handcuffs. The thick-necked French thugs and Luca the scrawny thief were jostled out next, each hollering in his respective language. Cambriolage just shook his head, as if it were all so terribly inconvenient and, thanks to the police, he was going to miss his evening cognac.

Ginevra was the last to go, looking scornful and tragic. She held Beatrice's gaze as a young cop escorted her out. "I was a victim of circumstance," she declared. "You'll see. I'll prove my innocence."

Beatrice stared after her former teacher with a combination of anger and pity until the chief investigator interrupted her thoughts, asking where they could find the *real* turtles.

She had imagined opening the secret passageway so many times that she didn't even have to think. She strode to the corner of the library, behind a massive antique globe. She scoured the shelves but it didn't take long to find the slim copy of Aristotle. As confidently as if she'd done it dozens of times before, she tugged the volume beside it, and just like Caterina had described in the diary, a section of the shelves swung open. The officers, Marco, Mr. Archer, even old Signora Costaguti, stared into the cavernous opening in stunned silence.

Beatrice described to the officers as best she could the location of the tunnel where she'd been forced to abandon the turtles. "But you might want to bring some pretty powerful lamps and a pair of sniffer dogs while you're at it. It's a pitch-black maze down there."

Then, inevitably, came the question Beatrice had

been dreading: "How did you know where to find them?" Marco translated, shooting her a warning look.

Beatrice paused. She couldn't reveal she'd stolen a four-hundred-year-old diary and found a hand-drawn treasure map. Not only did it sound incredibly far-fetched—the kind of thing grown-ups never believe— but the last thing she wanted was to get in trouble, especially now that she was practically a hero.

Everyone stared at her expectantly. Finally, Marco broke the silence.

"I helped her," he said.

Beatrice whipped her head around. She wasn't sure whether to be grateful he was protecting her, or resentful he was taking the credit.

"You see," he began, "my father owns an antique shop, and we have documents on all the palaces in town, especially the ones built on top of ruins. We found an old map of the ancient theater under the Mattei Palace, and Beatrice guessed the turtles were down there. I never thought she'd go looking for them, though!"

Beatrice let out a silent sigh of relief when Marco's explanation seemed to satisfy the police. Her father's narrowed eyes, however, said he knew it wasn't the whole story, and he'd be expecting the full version later.

The chief investigator and Marco exchanged a few words. "He wants to know if we have any idea who Cambriolage was working for," Marco translated. "He says that if all these thefts really are connected, they have the chance to uncover the biggest art crime ring in decades."

"Oh, I don't think that'll be too hard to figure out," Beatrice drawled.

Eyebrows raised all around.

"Well," she said slowly, as if she were helping a group of three-year-olds work out two plus two, "who works in the biggest, most luxurious palace in Rome?"

Blank stares.

"A palace designed by Michelangelo with frescoes by Carracci . . . ?"

"Palazzo Farnese! The—the French ambassador?" said her father, aghast.

Beatrice nodded, unable to suppress a grin. "And I know for a fact that he's behind not just this, but several recent disappearances around the city."

"And how did you discover all this?"

She couldn't tell whether her dad was impressed or appalled.

"More important," interrupted the investigator, by way of his young interpreter, "how do you intend to prove it?"

In lieu of an answer, she looked pointedly at Cambriolage's phone.

Really, what would they do without her?

thirty-two

UNEXPECTED GIFTS

Beatrice and Marco were holed up in the café on Via del Portico d'Ottavia, waiting out a sudden rainstorm. It had made a mess of Beatrice's white canvas sandals, but she was grateful all the same for a bit of relief from the heat.

They scoured the papers for mention of their nighttime adventures, but couldn't find a single word. It must've happened too late to make the morning press. Still, the neighborhood was abuzz with talk of the dreadful act of vandalism that had occurred in the piazza.

Despite sleeping like the dead until well past noon,

Beatrice's insides still fizzed with leftover adrenaline. She couldn't resist rehashing the night's events with Marco, but there was something between them that remained unspoken.

Beatrice plucked up the courage to broach the subject. "Marco?"

"Yeah?" He looked up from the paper.

"Well, I just wanted to say that . . . I mean, you should know that . . . I'm sorry I suspected you."

"I was wondering when you'd say that!"

"Well, I *am* sorry!" She crossed her arms in a huff.

"Hey, I was only joking," he said, cracking a dimpled grin.

Beatrice smiled too, relieved he didn't hold it against her.

"I understand; you barely knew me. And I'm sorry I didn't believe you about the fakes. I guess I just thought I knew better, being Roman and all."

She cocked her left eyebrow, a hint of a smile on her lips. "I guess I showed you."

"And to think, all along, your Italian teacher was behind the whole thing."

"I know. She's so passionate about art; it's hard to believe she would conspire to steal it." She shook her head with a despondent smile. "Now I really have no hope of learning Italian before school starts."

"I can teach you," Marco suggested, as if he were offering to do nothing more time-consuming than tie her shoe.

"Yeah, right." She chuckled. Her eyes flicked over to his, but he wasn't laughing. "You'd do that?"

"Sure, why not?" He shrugged. "I mean, I've been speaking Italian since birth; how hard can it be to teach someone else?"

"I warn you: I'm a very slow learner."

"Somehow I doubt that."

Beatrice wasn't positive, but she thought, just maybe, she detected a trace of admiration.

"I still can't believe you broke into that palace on your own. Weren't you scared you'd get caught?"

"Of course I was scared, but I didn't have a choice. By the way, thanks for covering for me. I didn't know how the police would react if they knew I'd taken the diary."

"No worries. So, are you going to keep it?"

"No. I ended up telling my dad the whole story. He's taking it back today."

"That's a bummer."

"Well, I did always say I was just *borrowing* it. It doesn't belong to me, and if I kept it, I wouldn't be any better than them, would I?"

"Beatrice, it's a diary, not a priceless work of art."

"I know. But it's not mine," she said simply. Then an impish look spread across her face. "I did save one thing, though. Such a teeny, tiny, little thing, I don't think anyone will ever notice."

She reached into her bag and pulled out an old yellowed document in a protective plastic sleeve.

"Wow, what is that? The map?" Marco eyed it eagerly.

Beatrice nodded as she unfolded it slowly, enjoying his anticipation. She spread it out on the table and Marco bent to study it.

"This is so awesome!" he said.

Beatrice watched his eyes soak up every line, his fingers caress the yellowed parchment. She decided to do something rash.

"I want you to have it."

"What?"

"You heard me. I want you to have the map."

"Beatrice! You can't do that! You already gave back

the diary. You can't give this away too!"

"Yes I can, and I want to. You appreciate it more than I do; it's obvious. Just promise me you'll never put it up for sale," she added, her eyes brimming with mirth.

"Never!" He grinned, the hint of a blush showing through his tanned cheeks. An instant later, the grin was gone and he turned his liquid brown eyes on hers. *"Grazie, Beatrice."*

It was the first time he'd said her name the Italian way, and her stomach did a little flip. *"Prego,"*[1] she said shyly. "If I hadn't had your help, I'd never have been able to save the turtles, or the other works of art on Cambriolage's list."

Neither of them said anything for a long moment. Finally Beatrice broke the silence.

"You know, I did it all for selfish reasons, of course."

"What do you mean?"

"I wanted to be able to look out my bedroom window and see that fountain—Bernini's turtles and all—every morning and every night."

· ·

1. "You're welcome."

They both laughed at the absurdity of this statement, even though there was a nugget of truth to it.

"*Ciao, principessa*," said Mr. Archer, poking his head into Beatrice's room a few hours later.

"Hey, Dad. Where've you been?"

"Well, I took back the diary, and wouldn't you know it? There was an auction going on."

"Oh, that's right, I almost forgot!" Beatrice closed her book and hopped off the bed. "How was it?"

"Pretty impressive. There was some highly valuable merchandise."

"Anything we could afford?" she asked hopefully.

"Maybe." He frowned ambiguously and walked out of the room.

Beatrice chased him into the living room. "You can't keep me in suspense, Dad! Did you get something?"

"Well . . . ," he said with a teasing smile, "I did get one *little* thing."

"Really? What is it? Show me! Show me! Show me!" She jumped up and down with delight.

"Now, before you get too excited," he cautioned, "it's very small. Rather insignificant, really. In fact,

I'm not even sure you'll like it."

"WHAT IS IT?" She could bear the suspense no longer.

The corners of his mouth twitched and his eyes flicked to the right. Beatrice followed his gaze to the portrait resting on the mantel over the fireplace. The portrait of Caterina.

Beatrice gasped.

"Do you like it?"

"I can't believe it." She approached the painting. "Is she really ours?"

He nodded. "It seems the owners are in a desperate state. In trouble with the law, according to the rumors." His eyes gleamed. "The auctioneer was instructed to sell every last item, so the opening bids were slashed way down."

"But what made you get this one?" Did he know? *How* did he know?

"I couldn't say. Something just drew me to it."

A chill ran down Beatrice's spine.

"Plus, there's something about it—the nuance of light and shadow—that reminds me of the work of my favorite painter, Caravaggio. He was your mother's favorite too. The canvas is terribly dirty, but after a good cleaning, I think it'll be even more remarkable."

Beatrice stared up at the portrait. She still couldn't believe it was theirs.

"It's uncanny how much you remind me of her."

"The woman in the portrait?"

"No, silly." He stood behind her, placing his chin on the top of her head as they gazed at the painting together. "Your mother."

"Really?" She looked up at him, her eyes wide. He never talked about her mother.

"She was passionate about art, like you. For her, art was sacred and to be protected at any cost. She would have done *anything* to save those turtles, just like you did. Despite the fact that you broke about a thousand rules and put yourself in unspeakable danger—and don't think you're out of hot water for that—she would have been very proud of you. I should have listened to you from the beginning. Your bravery and smarts saved more than just those turtles, and this city owes you—big-time. Not to mention your old dad. If it weren't for you, I'd have lost my job," he said simply.

With her father's words warming her from the inside out, Beatrice contemplated the painting. Somehow, in this new setting, illuminated by the summer light streaming in from the window, Caterina's face didn't seem quite so sad. From her position above the fireplace, Caterina gazed out of the frame, through the window, and across the square toward the palace where she once had lived. The palace that had witnessed her miserable existence, so many years ago. The palace that had seen the utter ruin of its greedy owners at last.

Was it Beatrice's imagination, or could she detect a slightly different expression on Caterina's face? Was it—could it be—a look of triumph?

ACKNOWLEDGMENTS

I am forever indebted to my brilliant and tireless agent, John Silbersack, for his insight, warmth, wisdom, and experience, and for finding the perfect home for my book. Thanks as well to everyone at Trident Media Group, especially Caitlin Meuser.

Immense gratitude to the marvelous team at HarperCollins Children's: Deborah Murphy, Rebecca Frumento, Alana Whitman, and Jen Klonsky for all their hard work and for making me feel so welcome; Elizabeth Lynch for answering my incessant questions and offering much-needed advice; Kathryn Silsand and Jacqueline Hornberger for their impeccable and meticulous copyediting skills; and Alison Klapthor and Becca Stadtlander for creating quite possibly the most gorgeous book cover I've ever seen. Particular thanks to my editor, Kristen Pettit, for believing in this book and helping to transform it into the best version of itself.

Love and thanks to my mother, Patricia Morosic, for teaching me to go after my dreams, and to my father, Sam Parks, for instilling in me his love of books. Thank you also to Don Morosic and Bobbie "Big Apple Bob" Parks, for being just about the greatest stepparents a girl could ask for. Thank you to Kendra Pieroni, Robin Clover, Samantha Pitts, Tia Parks, and Monique Schiff for always humoring their dreamy and dramatic little sister, and for supplying me with a dozen ready-made readers in the form of my beloved nieces and nephews.

Tante grazie to Luisa Abate for keeping my fat pregnant feet as cool as possible during the hottest summer in Italian history while I frantically revised against a merciless biological deadline. Thanks as well to the entire Ianniello clan, my second family, and in particular to Elisa Ianniello, the first child to hear Beatrice's story (and who always pronounced her name in the deliciously Italian way).

Inexpressible gratitude to Suzanne Morrison and Katy Sewall, without whom this book literally would not have been published. Their indefatigable advice, insight, enthusiasm, encouragement, and faith will never, ever be forgotten. Enormous thanks to Rmishka "Burnsie" Singh, Lisa Chambers, Julie MacKenzie, and Claudia Casagrande for reading early drafts and giving invaluable feedback. Special thanks to my youngest beta readers, Giulia and Paloma Martinez-Brenner, for offering the tween expat perspective.

Heartfelt thanks to Maeve Högland for being my champion, cheerleader, and one-woman fan club. Many thanks also to Elizabeth Baker, Alexandra Bruzzese, Ryan Cofrancesco, Amy Knauff, Linda Martinez, and Jenni Woodward for their unfaltering encouragement and support during the long years of writing and revising this book. Extra special thanks to India Badiner, who, when I met her, was a thirteen-year-old girl living in Piazza Mattei with a view of the Turtle Fountain out her bedroom window.

Eternal love and gratitude to my husband, Claudio Ianniello, for always believing in me, encouraging me, and pushing me to persevere (not to mention giving me plot ideas when I was stuck and ready to dump the entire manuscript in the trash); and to Aurelio Samuel, my own little redhead and good luck charm.

AUTHOR'S NOTE

The actual history, art, and architecture of the city of Rome inspired *Midnight in the Piazza*. Every building, monument, and street in the book are faithful to reality, from the Portico of Octavia to, of course, Piazza Mattei and the Turtle Fountain. Likewise, all the works of art mentioned in the book exist, with the exception of the portrait of Duchess Caterina.

Palazzo Giacomo Mattei (and the three other palaces that make up Isola Mattei) were indeed built upon the ruins of the ancient Theater of Balbus. According to popular local legend, the late-sixteenth-century Duke Muzio Mattei did in fact build the Turtle Fountain in one night in order to impress his future father-in-law. And while Muzio Mattei is a historical figure, his tragic bride, Caterina, as well as the troubles of the modern-day Mattei family, come from my imagination.

To discover more about the places Beatrice visits in Rome, check out www.tiffany-parks.com/beatrices-rome.